HARMONY

BOOK ONE OF THE SONG OF THE SEA

HARMONY

illustrated
by
Michael
Casad

by
Stephen E.
Cosgrove

Graphic Arts Center Publishing Company

Portland, Oregon

International Standard Book Number 1-55868-008-X
Library of Congress Number 89-83842
Text © MCMLXXXIX by Stephen E. Cosgrove
Illustrations © MCMLXXXIX by Michael Casad
All rights reserved.
No part of this book can be reproduced by any means
without written permission of the publisher.
Published by Graphic Arts Center Publishing Company
P.O. Box 10306 • Portland, Oregon 97210 • 503/226-2402
Editor-in-Chief • Douglas A. Pfeiffer
Associate Editor • Jean Andrews
Designer • Becky Gyes
Typographer • Harrison Typesetting
Color House • Spectrum West
Printer • Dynagraphics, Inc.
Bindery • Lincoln & Allen
Printed in the United States of America

Dedicated to my loving wife, Shaerie,
who sang with me three years ago on Patrick's Point,
the beginning of the Song of the Sea. She sings always in my heart.
This, the first book, is yours.

Stephen

CONTENTS

GLOSSARY OF TERMS

THE DEEP — *All the waters below the surface of the sea.*

DOLPHINS — *The delight and laughter in the sea. Brethren to the whale.*

THE DRYSIDE — *The land and winds that blow above and beyond the sea.*

FEATHERED FURIES — *An assortment of aquatic birds, especially seagulls and pelicans, who scavenge for their food.*

FLIPPER-FINS — *Seals and their pups. Brethren to the whale.*

GOLDEN LIGHT — *The light of day.*

POD — *A group or gathering of whales who live their lives in community.*

SANDWALKERS — *Man.*

SHELL-SHARKS — *All forms of boats and ships that carry sandwalkers across the sea.*

SILVERSIDE — *Dark or moonlit nights.*

THE SONG — *The history of the pod as it is recorded by the scribe. The song is all that happens and has happened to the pod since the beginning.*

TIDES — *Two tides equal one day.*

WATERS OF LIFE — *All the salt waters that make up the seas and oceans of the world.*

WHALE — *For the purpose of this story, a variety of whales was developed to create one fictitious pod. A bit of Orca, a smattering of Beluga, and the amazing songs as sung by the Humpback.*

THE WHALES

CACOPHONY   *(Ke kaf' e ne) A bull in the pod who grows to be its largest member.*

HARMONY   *Born the first white whale in the history of the pod.*

MELODY   *Born a little before Harmony, her voice is sweet and true.*

METRONOME   *A young whale never to lead, always to follow.*

NARWHAL OF THE HORN   *Mystical whales who are now thought to be extinct.*

PERCUSSION   *A young cow, all rhythm, no rhyme.*

PHILOSOPHY   *The oldest member of the pod whose charge is to create the theme of the song and keep it true to its original intent.*

RHAPSODY   *The mother of Harmony.*

TYMPANI   *(Tim' pa ne) The scribe, singer, and recorder of the Song of the Sea.*

*"Like a wave crashing on the coral sands . . .
so shall ye become part and measure of the Song of the Sea. "*
as sung to the pod by
Philosophy
in the tide 5345

PRELUDE

As this was the end, so it is the beginning. I float. I gently swim. I have nowhere to go. I have everywhere I should be. I am empty, yet filled with the final Song of the Sea. I am memory waiting for one last thought before I, too, will be forgotten.

I am called Harmony, the great white whale.

My tears mingle with the waters of life. I am the last living whale of my pod, for the others have all died and gone away. My family is gone. My friends are gone. My enemy is dead. She who loved me through all the silver tides is but a coda to this Song of the Sea. For I am Harmony, the last whale of my kind and I must sing the final song or not remember. I choose not to forget.

My song began simply . . .

I was calved some seventy-five hundred tides before, in a time when the waters were mirror smooth and I lay still in the darkness. My sanctuary, the womb, was the lull before the storm of life. I could hear no sound but the beating of two hearts and a low, gentle roar.

There was a singleness in the two of us.

Then, in a burst of bubbles and an explosion of light, I was thrust upon the world, and the world upon me. Spinning round and round, I felt a terrible wrenching agony as the cord of life was broken for all eternity.

I screamed. I moaned. But as the waters of life gently washed me clean, I regained my senses and began to look around. Lo, what a world! It moved. It surged. It washed and gurgled about me. It was quiet. It was cool. Yet, it was warm. It was all things in opposition. It was paradox. It was the sea, the beginning, the end.

Light. The golden light danced upon the waves and burned into my memory, visions I would never again see in quite the same way. Above me, an expanse of blue stretched from one side of the sea to the other with strange bits of white fluff and foam hanging there, suspended, waiting for a breeze to carry them to some distant home. The world I lay upon turned me this way and that. Everywhere I looked, all was the same, yet different. Bright, light blue. Stark, bright white. Gently, the world breathed upon me as I saw all that I could see.

Winged, feathered furies began to fly by me, buoyed by a gentle breeze. They heeled and reeled, swimming in the air like winged poems of great beauty. Then, one by one, they began to scream noisily and swooped down, pecking at my yet gentle flesh and jabbing at my eyes. One, then another—they were everywhere, stabbing and pulling.

I had to escape! With fear in my heart, I sank and fell into the world. Falling, falling, gently falling. Colors, bright colors muted by the water, wiggled and wriggled about, for all around me were the fishes of the sea. I smiled and wanted to share this with *She* who used to be part of me, but now *She* was gone. This caused me to cry in anguish, but the tears brought no relief. Still I fell through the world—down and down, round and round, deeper and deeper.

The light changed from bright to dim, and dimmer still. I could see a mountainous, shadowy shape moving before me as if it were alive. I looked, and then looked again. That was no mountain before me, and it really was alive!

With a gasp, I took a deep breath and nearly died, for even the air was changed and had turned against me. With a cough and a gag, I expelled the evil air, but now there was nothing left to breathe! Helplessly, I sank lower and lower into the world. Behind me, the monstrous creature followed me down and down, to watch me drown.

Just as all was fading, I was lifted, as if by some miracle, back into the world of light and bright. With a fearful gasp, I breathed deep and found the world turned soft again, but the mountain of flesh was still there before me. I turned quickly, and there was another and another and another! They were everywhere with their slick, black, wrinkled skins. Big brown eyes were staring— staring at me. I bumped into them all as I vainly tried to escape.

Then, like musical chimes, laughter rang throughout all the waters of life. At first, it

Then, in a burst of bubbles and an explosion of light,
I was thrust upon the world,
and the world upon me . . .

frightened me, but slowly it began to buff the sharp edge from my fear. Although I began to giggle with it, I still was surrounded by the monstrous shapes that penned me in, and this caused my eyes to open wide.

I again sought escape, but a most melodious voice called my name, "Harmony, beautiful white whale, why do you run?"

I froze. The voice was music, and it knew my name. But what could it be? I remembered the sound but it was different somehow.

I twisted to look at part of myself and I was white, therefore I must be whale. But what was whale and who was speaking to me in a voice I knew so well but could not see?

I sang out in frustration as my eyes filled with salty tears, "Who are you that sings to me? I know you, yet I know you not."

Laughter's musical sound washed over and around me like a wet-water wave. I was so startled by the closeness of the sound that I sought once again to escape into the deep. But this time, the mountains of slick, black flesh pressed against me and held me tight. I wiggled this way and that, using all the strength at my call, but to no avail. I tried to lift myself up into the dryside, but I was trapped.

Then again the voice, "Do not fear, my little Harmony. I am your mother, Rhapsody."

I looked about, but still saw only high, black walls of flesh. "Mother, mother! Where are you? I look but I cannot see!"

Once again, laughter danced upon the waters, shaking the flesh that held me fast. Slowly, the black wall before me opened up, and there blinked a most enormous and beautiful eye.

I stared into that eye and saw there the clear reflection of a tiny white whale. But what held my attention was not the little whale that I knew was me, but rather that great eye, the gentle eye that would always be able to look into my very soul, the eye of my mother, Rhapsody.

That tide and the next and the next were filled with rapt wonderings. I learned how to breathe the soft, sweet air of the sky above and how to sound, to seek the deep, cool waters below. I stretched and moved the muscles of my soon-to-be mighty body. I learned to swim and move my tail to move faster. I learned to flip my flippers to guide me round and round or straight ahead in powerful bursts.

I learned of the whale. I learned that I was an oddity—a rare and wondrous occurrence—for I was born white. I learned as I listened to the songs that all whales sing: tales of this and tales of that, places to go, places that had never been seen before. All was sung in beautiful melody and lilting note.

The tides passed one hundred times and then many, many more as I grew older and bolder. Soon I took to swimming gentle forays into the surrounding seas but always near the guardian eye of my mother or the other adults of the pod. Stronger and stronger I became, slowly breaking even the emotional ties that bonded me to my mother. One day as I was swimming, skimming the surface foam, I bumped quite innocently into a young whale much larger than I. Suddenly, without warning, I was flipped unceremoniously onto my back and buffeted about in the churning waters. Over and over again, I was flipped and rolled, and though I tried to turn and race away, this bull of a whale seemed obsessed with my destruction. He rammed my sides repeatedly and bellowed, "You will respect the waters in which I swim. You will not foul the waters in which I swim. Remember, and never forget that I am Cacophony, he that rules the sea!" His song was loud and discordant, lacking all form of melody. The attack was finally broken off when a sweeter song was sung, "Cacophony! Leave him be! Yours is not the only song of the sea. He bumped into you quite innocently. I was watching and I did see!"

As the noise breaker swam away, I was surrounded by other whales my own age and size. They gleefully bumped and rubbed against me. As youngsters do, we all quickly became fast friends: Percussion, a noisy lady, but a lady just the same; Metronome, softly spoken but always in rhythm and perfect rhyme; plump Adagio's song was ponderously slow; and finally, Melody, the one whose voice had saved me from a battering. She was the prettiest whale of all—soft of eye and song.

The others marveled at my white skin, but the oddity quickly passed, as do all things of youth, as we played and frolicked in the sea.

Likewise, I soon passed from my mother's milk, and the bond between us began to fade. I spent more and more time with the others my age, and we learned together. And as we learned, the memories of the early days seemed to fade away, crowded deep by new memory and new learning.

Once, as I rushed to my mother to drink some lunch, I was offered instead a small silvered fish, long since finished with life. What fun, what delight! A new toy. I grabbed the fish by the tail and rushed about on a passing wave. I dove into the deep, thrashing my head from side to side and nearly banging myself in the eye with this new plaything.

On and on I played, until finally I came to the surface, where I tossed the toy up into the dryside and caught it as it fell. Splash roll and crash, I thrashed about the waters shredding it to unrecognizable condition. Finally, I threw it high into the air and dashed to catch it. I waited, but fall it did not. I cast my eye to the sky and looked about the dryside, but there was no toy falling, falling to the sea to play with me. Instead, there were the horrid feathered furies eating my toy.

I was mad. I was furious. These feathered monsters were destroying my very first toy. I charged into them as they floated on the silken seas and they fluttered and squawked out of the water. As they flapped and fluttered, they carried my toy away. I gave chase but soon they were fatter, and my toy was gone.

I rushed back to my mother lamenting my loss. She chuckled and softly sang, "No, my dear sweet Harmony, that was not a toy to be played with. That was food to be eaten to help you grow with the sea."

It seemed a bit confusing to me. Food before had always come from mother. The toy, or rather the fish, had come from mother but was not a part of her. Milk was food; fish were fun, and now fish were to be food and not fun? Odd, to say the least.

Mother flicked her flukes and disappeared deep for a moment, reappearing with a new toy, or rather food. "Now, my Harmony, don't play with this, you must eat it!"

"Oh, yuck! Eat a fish! Eat a fellow form from the sea?"

"Fear not, my son. We take from the sea to become part of the sea. The fish live to eat and be eaten. Eat now, and then you shall see."

I closed my eyes, opened my mouth and swallowed this part of all that was around me. Unfortunately, I swallowed nearly as much water and coughed and hacked, but surprisingly, this tiny morsel was sweet, and I found myself wanting to taste more.

Mother dove, and I followed. With mighty twists of her body, she silently glided down near some flickering, flashing forms. "Wow, look at all the food!" I sang in glee. I rushed into the mass of fish, but just like that, in an explosion of silver and blues, they were gone. I looked about and found another flickering mass and charged, but they, too, scattered like so much kelp in a stormy sea.

*I charged into them
as they floated on the silken seas . . .*

Mother patiently watched and only interfered to teach me the delicate ways of hunting the seas. She taught me to slip quietly into a school of fish and then quickly to catch. She taught me patience and waiting so that the fish would come to me.

That day, I ate for the first time from the sea. I learned that the harder a fish is to catch, the sweeter the meat. But the sweeter the meat, the harder the fish was to catch. I was fast; some of the fishes were faster. But I ate and ate until my belly swelled, ached, and I could eat no more.

I was so full that I could barely float, feeling as if I were filled with stones. My mother laughed and left me to my misery singing, "You must take from the sea only that which you need—no more, no less! If you take more, there will be less, and eventually nothing will be left in the sea and you, my child, will be very hungry. But take less and there will always be more." With that, she left me with my lesson, learned in a swirl of bubbles and an aching tummy, soon to heal with rest in the sea.

The next golden light and the next, I hunted the seas, becoming more and more independent of all those things that my mother provided. Soon I began to hunt with the others my age, and together we found sweet fishes to fill our bellies.

One day, we were joined by the great bellower and bully, Cacophony. "You bits of stick only search for minnows and clacker-claws," he sang in his racking voice. "Come with me and I'll show you how to find the bigger fish. I do not eat a hundred tiny fish to make a meal, I eat but one that fills me full." With that, he haughtily swam into the murk of the deep, assuming correctly that we would meekly follow.

Now I don't think that Cacophony had really fished for bigger fishes in the sea, but he had opened his big mouth and now had to see just what would swim in. We followed him about and around the seas. We passed many groups and schools of sweet-meated fish: tuna-tail, bug-eye and flat-tail, but Cacophony disdained them all as being too small. We dove and we searched with this great hunter of the sea.

Soon before us was a sleek fish that circled idly in the waters. His snout was nearly pointed, and a large arcing fin traced a trail on the surface of the sea. "You know," I sang a bit nervously, "it seems that mother did sing to me about this fellow from the sea. Mother sang about the finned one. 'For the sharper the fin, the sharper the teeth; the sharper the teeth, the harder the fish are to eat.'"

"Oh, that is just carp bile," Cacophony sang cockily off tune. "This long-finned fish shall be my meal." With that he began his attack. No finesse, no circling to confuse his prey, Cacophony charged straight at this steely-eyed fish who didn't run like other fishes. This fish just stared stupidly as the large whale attacked.

The finned fish was not so stupid, as he was arrogant. Cacophony swam closer, his jaws extended, hopefully to swallow this fish in one great bite, but as he drew down, the fish turned and seemed to smile evilly. This fish didn't wish to be eaten.

The attacker soon became the attacked, as this finned and slick-skinned serpent snaked about and opened his mouth. Rows upon rows of glistening, sharpened teeth lined his upper and lower jaws. He was quicker than quick and sliced at Cacophony. The first time, he missed, and the great whale turned to escape, but the finned monster slid silkily by, slicing a cut from his mouth to his eye. The water filled with red-brown sweetness, and without fear, the rest of our young pod rushed to the rescue.

I am sure it was not by design that we saved Cacophony, but more surprise than fear shocked this sharp-fin from his meal as we surged upon him. He saucily twisted his tail, and without concern, as if nothing had happened at all, slipped away into the deep.

We gathered about Cacophony as we swam back to the main body of the pod. The older whale sang nothing, filled with fear, I am sure. But as we swam, the stinging salty waters of life cured the cut and the bleeding stopped.

As we neared the shadowy shapes of the pod, Cacophony twisted from our group and sang loudly, "Why did you stop him? I was letting him attack to get him closer. You jelly fish ruined my

hunt!" With that, he bulled his way from our midst and swam away from the pod to sulk.

We couldn't help at first being shocked by our sudden change from heroes to hinderers, but I think all of us realized this was Cacophony's way of thanking us for saving him from a slashing death. None of us ever spoke of it again, although it was recorded forever in the Song of the Sea.

The tides passed quickly, and the golden light became hotter and brighter as the pod slowly began migrating, following the sweet taste and tease of cold waters. Lo, what wondrous things to see! There were great storms and all sorts of winged feathered furies that flew. There were bits of this and bits of that floating in the sea, smelling of strange new worlds yet to be discovered. We never stopped for long, only to eat and rest.

Every night, as golden light turned to silverside and black, the bulk of the pod rested, tired from the day's journey. We, the young ones, would all gather about our enforced leader—Cacophony, the bellower. His song was raucous, but strangely compelling. He teased and bullied us all mercilessly for anything and everything he thought we had done during the day. Then he would make up a game, and we would frolic and play—but by his rules, which always ended with, ". . . and Cacophony wins!"

One silverside tide, we all gathered, as was our custom, away from the feeding pod. We floated and rocked on the surface telling tales of the day's journey. Cacophony, quieter than usual, silently disappeared beneath the sea. Suddenly the waters erupted as Cacophony crashed into our midst. Then, just as abruptly, he disappeared again.

Over and over, he leaped high into the air as we looked on in admiration and envy. Finally, I followed to watch as Cacophony dropped like a rock through the water. With a mighty flip of his tail and the muscular pulling of his flukes, he shot up through the world. Eagerly, I imitated his moves and found myself quite unexpectedly launched out of the sea.

The dryside surrounded me as I saw my pod of friends below. Then my flight came to an abrupt end, as I crashed heavily back down into the world. I vented and dove, breaching again and again, a little higher each time. Cacophony followed, and the sea was filled with our song of delight.

Our frolicking caused the feathered furies to gather, and they wheeled about the dry sky, searching for some opportunistic meal. Suddenly, I breached so high that all of me left the

world, and I found myself eye-to-eye with one of the feathered flesh-eaters. I opened my mouth and snapped tightly on this creature whose brothers had caused me so much fear on the day of my birth. For, you see, I had a plan, a marvelous plan—I hoped to show this feathery thing the wet side of the world and to see how well he flew beneath the water. Instead, all that remained was a mouthful of tail feathers, and the rest went screeching away.

By now, the whole pod was flying in the air, breaching high, reaching for the sky. The world was filled with giggles, bubbles, laughter, and froth. All of the whales were breaching, save one, the pudgy whale called Adagio. Try though he did, Adagio could not breach through the world into the dryside.

Cacophony then began to swim round and round berating the chubby whale. But no matter how hard he tried, Adagio could not breach and finally rested at the surface, his eyes glazed from exertion. Then, without warning, he rose into the air with a "whoosh." Cacophony had breached below him, ramming him out of the world and into the sky above.

Adagio's eyes, at first wide with fear, squinted in twinkles of joy, as Cacophony breached beneath him again and again. Over and over, Adagio was hurled into the dryside.

But a strange melody began moaning

Drawing all of my fear into strength,
I lashed my tail as he passed
and smashed him full in the face . . .

in the sea. Quiet first, then louder, it was a harsh, metallic noise full of disharmony—a song not right with the world. It was a tune, yet not quite a song, a buzzing, a roar. The adult pod called us back to the deep, away from the surface, "Come, little ones, come!" they sang urgently. "The sand-walkers approach on their shell-sharks that hum!"

One by one, we began to drift slowly down into the world and safety: Melody, Percussion, Metronome, and I. But Adagio stayed at the surface, for he heard neither the cries of warning nor the harsh grating song that approached. He was the slow one; the thrill of being blasted into the air by Cacophony had dulled his senses. Slowly it began to dawn on him that there was danger. As he started to drop into the world and safety, he was again popped back to the light by the obsessed older whale. With fear building like a song that must be sung, he tried to dive again and again. But each time he tried, Cacophony shoved him up into the dryside.

The game had worn thin, and Adagio's pleasure turned to pain as he was rammed over and over. The water filled with a screaming, the nearly roaring sound of shell-sharks as they raced closer and closer. Cacophony sang loudly as he rammed the helpless smaller whale, "Nothing to fear, fat whale. Nothing to fear . . . no time for tears!" Once again, he rammed the pudgy little whale viciously out of the world, just as the first of two shell-sharks screamed across the surface and raced on past. The water churned, turning all to confusion, as the shell-shark ripped across the back of Adagio and then callously sped away.

As quickly as the scare had begun, so was it over. The shell-sharks disappeared, and their harsh droning turned to silence. The world softened once again, and the froth turned to wave. Relieved, we surfaced, laughing at our escape. Adagio floated nearby; his eyes were still glazed with fright.

Something was very wrong. Adagio, softly first, then louder, began screaming a song of pain. The other young whales and I rushed to him, and only then did we realize that the sea was turning red from the deep slices across his back! His song stopped as suddenly as it started, and he began to fall into the sleep of the deep. We all pressed close to him, holding his limp form above the world so he could breathe. Like the clanging of rock on rock, we sang a song of fear as the pod raced to our aid.

Wispy mists of clouds began to gather on the darkening horizon of the world as we supported Adagio. Winds from the dryside began to whip the sea into an angry froth as we rocked on the waves as one. Cacophony circled about us, crying out, "Let him sink into the deep! Let him fall into the final sleep!"

Though he taunted and railed, we continued to press inward passing our warmth and life into the unconscious Adagio. At last, we could hear the mass of the pod calling for us to hold on. My mother, Rhapsody, broke the surface of the world near us and offered her bulk to relieve some of the younger whales from Adagio's weight.

Rhapsody sang in staccato form, "How did this happen? Who does know? Why did not Adagio hide where you others did go?"

Melody, Percussion, Metronome, and I all remained silent. No song did we sing as we looked, waiting. Then, Cacophony began to sing in his crude, raking voice, "It was the bright one . . . the white one, who forced Adagio to stay. It was Harmony! It was Harmony who wouldn't let him swim away!"

I started to object, but was curtly stopped by my mother who sang, "My son, I will deal with you later in the deep. For now—silence—so the injured one can sleep. He will live, though scarred by what he has seen. In time, it will only appear as a silverside dream!"

It was then that Adagio opened his pain-filled eyes. Haltingly, he sang a simple song, "It was not Harmony . . . It was the other, the one called . . ." At that moment, whether by accident or design, Cacophony, buoyed by a storm-whipped wave, came crashing down on Adagio's head, shoving him back down into the world. Cacophony's massive body lay passively on Adagio, forcing the life from his lungs.

I understood what Cacophony was attempting to do, and I rammed at his side, vainly trying to break Adagio free. I hammered and hammered, finally bowling the larger whale off Adagio's still form. Cacophony, in fear of being further implicated, sounded deep and soon was lost from sight at the bottom of the world's gloom. In a blind rage, I followed him, diving deeper than I had ever dived before.

Finally, near the bottom of the world I found Cacophony, or rather Cacophony found me. Out of the murkiness, he lunged, ramming his mighty head into my side, rolling me over and over. Before I could recover, he attacked again and again. Finally drawing all of my fear into strength, I lashed my tail as he passed and smashed him full in the face. He was stunned, and before he could return to the attack again, I charged and rammed his exposed flank. Bubbles burst from his mouth, more from the shock than pain.

Suddenly, the fight was stopped by a voice singing clearly in the deep, "Your violence must stop, for you are fighting in vain. Adagio is already dead!"

All of the pent-up anger within me vented like soiled air, and I went limp. With a final blow, Cacophony slapped me viciously, and then he was gone. So dazed was I that as a new form appeared I tensed for battle.

"Fear not. I am Tympani. Recorder for a time of the Song of the Sea."

With a gentle flip of his tail, Tympani began the climb back to the golden light. Stiffly, I followed as I remembered my parent teaching me of Tympani, the recorder, the singer of the Song of the Sea.

We broke the surface together, and Tympani began to sing. He sang of the first tide, the beginning of the pod. He sang of all the beauty of the waves and the taste of the tides. He sang of the sandwalkers and their encroachment on all the great whales of the sea. He sang of the births, deaths, loves, and battles of the pod since the song began. With ghosting sounds echoing from the deep, other whales hesitantly joined in a chorus here and there. They sang through the births of the young whales and finally of Adagio's death, the final verse and measure, for now, in the Song of the Sea.

As Tympani finished, there was a low silence broken only by the lonely sound of the wind whispering over the waves. After a long silence to make sure there were no echoes to the song, I asked, "Why do we sing?"

The old whale chuckled and said, "The pod is like a song and it lives to be sung. Each whale plays an important role in the song. Symphony is the director, our leader who guides us where we go and at what tempo. Philosophy sets the mood for the song. He thinks wonderful thoughts, gives theme to all the music, and purpose to our being as well as to all creatures of the sea and sand."

From the deep, came the rumbling gastric mumblings of Cacophony, "Carp bile!"

Tympani ignored the interruption as he finished by explaining his own position as scribe, the recorder of the song for the pod. "And I, little Harmony, have the loneliest part of the song. For I must stand off and watch, listen and record the song as it is sung. No matter what disaster should befall the pod, I must not and cannot interfere. No matter what violence threatens the pod, whether by the waters of life themselves or by the lowly sandwalkers, the scribe must never be involved . . . he must never interfere. The scribe must only listen and remember the Song of the Sea and pass it on before he dies."

I was caught now—captured by the song and all its glorious melodies. "And who will you pass the song on to?" I asked.

The old whale paused in the water and floated quietly, "It is the tradition of the pod that positions of responsibility be passed on from father or mother to son or daughter. So by what has passed before, I must pass the song to my son." He paused, then continued, "However, my son carries but one melody. My son is . . . Cacophony!"

From the deep rolled oily, maniacal laughter.

IMPROVISATION

The tides passed quickly with the journey, and soon we reached the cool crisp waters where we whiled our time. The ocean was filled with life and the joy of our song. We, the young whales, grew, nearing adulthood but still relishing the value of play.

Here, there would always be food and friendship and a love of the sea.

We grew as we ate the wonderful variety of food that abounded in these waters. Tuna-tail and flipper-fin all made us fat and contented with the life we led. At times the stillness of the sea was broken by the irreverent humming of the shell-sharks, but they kept their distance and no one was harmed. It was a time in my life when I thought nothing would ever change.

But the sea was always moving, and with that movement came constant change. We had been in the frozen waters for nearly a hundred tides when there came the strangers who changed all of our lives forever. That tide, the golden lights turned to muted grey as water fell on water. Clouds skittered about at water's height, and there was no sky. It was a tide when I wished for nothing more than to fall asleep and wake to a crystal morning.

I had been at the outside of the pod, fishing for sweet meats in the sea. I was darting about, playing as much as hunting, when out of the murk of the deep came two ghostly forms, a silent bull whale and his mate. They were the first strangers I had ever met, although I had heard the faint song of other whales. They stood off frozen, etched in the crystal sea.

The female sang a gentle song with a lilting accent the likes that I had never heard before, "We two come as one. We come from a pod that is no more and never shall be. My mate was the recorder of all of the times the song was sung by our pod. He has reason now to sing to your scribe that which must be. He must sing his final song of the sea so that we may join the others." With that, she sang no more, and the two floated deathly still in the water.

I rushed through the pod searching all for the whereabouts of Tympani. I finally found him listening on the far side and quickly told him of the ghostly pair.

Tympani's eyes widened in understanding of this historic event. "This, my Harmony," he said, "is sad. For this scribe must sing a song of the end of all. He must sing of the end of his pod so that he too may have the end, the beginning. For a whale without song is a whale without reason for living. Come, you may listen, too, so that you might learn."

We swam through the pod to the frozen edge, and there, just as I had left them, were the two whales. Tympani approached slowly and then stopped and sang the gentle opening of our song. His singing was followed by the sweet lonely wail of the other scribe, as he countered with the opening to his song.

There was a pause, a blood-racing silence in the sea, and then the stranger continued, "I wish to sing my song. In singing my song I will pass it on to you and then I may end, so that I might begin again.

"Our pod began at the beginning, and it has swum the mighty waters of life recording all. There have passed many tides, and I am the twelfth and the last in a series of scribes that has recorded our song. Our song now ends in the glory of the end of all, to honor one who wished all to share in the end, the beginning."

He sang of great hunts, both in warm waters and cold. He sang of

adventure with the sandwalkers and their occasional attacks. He sang of strange lights on the dryside. He sang of good. He sang of evil. He sang of life and death in his pod. As the whale sang on and on, he always came back to what he sang as the honorable end . . . the THOUSAND DEATHS OF THE SANDWALKER, a symphony of a glorious death to honor another.

How long we floated and listened I do not know but this strange song told all the history of this unknown pod that now had ceased to be. Then, as the golden light began to change to the dark of the silverside, he sang these words I shall never forget, "But we are no more and never shall be, for we took upon us the honor and pledge of the THOUSAND DEATHS OF THE SANDWALKER as dreamed by the mystical Narwhal. Once we gave our pledge, we beached ourselves upon the shore so that we might die in honor of one whose end was near and to protest the encroachment of the sandwalkers on the sea."

"What are the mystical Narwhal?" I whispered to our scribe.

"Shh," said Tympani, "they are whale that no longer exist."

The other whale paused to sigh, then continued his song, "Our conductor, our leader of the pod and song, had done many things to honor us all. He had heard in a dream of the Narwhal, this tradition of all of the whales of a pod dying in a glorious death in protest of the sandwalker with one who had honored all. Our conductor was afraid, in part, of dying alone and asked us all to go with him to the end, the beginning. There is only one test to stop the THOUSAND

DEATHS OF THE SANDWALKER, and that is the sanity of him who asks. How there can be saneness in such a request, I do not know, but our leader was judged to be right with the world, and our pod agreed to join in this beaching . . . this protest to the sandwalkers on the dryside."

The two ghostly whales drew close to my side in the sea and sang this final stanza, "So they, the pod, raced to the shore and lifted themselves high into the dryside. And there, the voices mingled as one, and their pride was much as they died. Thus we sing our song. Thus we end our song. There is no more to our Song of the Sea."

The waters ran colder still as the final notes of this strange song echoed in the sea. The two floated oddly in the water. I looked and then looked again for there was no life in them. They had died while singing their song.

We floated in reverence near them, but we were gently interrupted by the old voice of Philosophy. "A strange ending to a song," he mused, "A very strange ending indeed. I must wonder on this. Is it good or is it bad? Is it right or is it mad? I wonder." With that, he swam away.

"But what of the Narwhal?" I asked again, awed by all that I had seen.

"The Narwhal lived long, long ago," patiently explained Tympani, "but it is sung that they were destroyed by the sandwalker and his march upon the sea. It is said that their ghosts wander the sea seeking revenge of the oddest sort against those who caused their extinction, which is . . . the THOUSAND DEATHS OF THE SANDWALKER."

We stayed for a time, then backed away as the two ghostly images dropped, swinging from side to side, into the waters deep, never to sing again.

It took many tides for the memory of that ghostly pair to fade, but like the morning mist, it burned thin and soon was gone.

One tide sometime later, as I swam dipping and diving, I rose to the surface and found myself surrounded by frozen walls of the waters of life. Everywhere I looked were reflections of me. Like an echo of light, many Harmonies bounced and glittered all around me. I forgot what I was chasing and sang simple songs that rang tinkling through the ice. I floated there for hours wrapped in the wonder of my conceit. The silverside night was magical, filled with myriad dancing lights that skipped along the sky in a profusion of magical colors, shimmering as if they were not there.

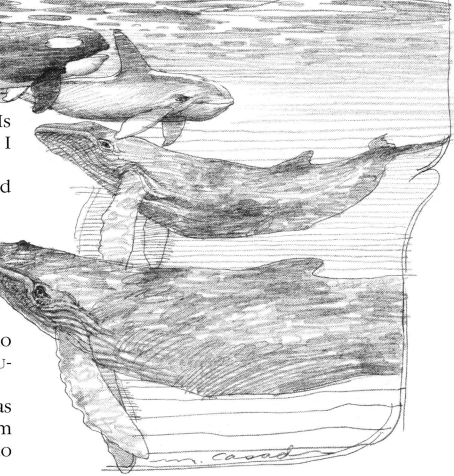

Finally, I realized I must return to the pod and dove down and under the crystal islands. With one eye cast above for the light, I continued diving but the crystal ice was always above me and I could not reach the dryside. I swam and I swam as my heart began to pound like a great drum in my ears. My lungs began to ache and draw in, taunting me with their need for air. I raced along, the ice ever present above. My reflection was a haunting image, laughing at me in my fear.

When I thought I could swim no more, I spied dancing lights on open water above. I surged and leaped up into the dryside blowing hard. Snow now stuttered about the sky. I sucked in great mouthfuls of the sweet air and slowly my heart stilled its hammering. I looked around but could see nothing of the pod, and new panic replaced old. Where was the pod?

I quieted my fears and listened, at first hearing nothing but the gentle wash of the sea. Then I began to hear the welcome sounds of whale nearby. Relieved, I swam back to my family and friends. The pod was already feeding, so I availed myself of a few of the sweet-meat tuna-tails that came my way. Soon, I found myself hunting in tandem with other members of the pod. I ate and ate, and soon I was once again satisfied with life.

I sang out in joy my simple song of adventure in the mirrored ice. I had just finished a stanza when I realized that no one else was singing. I stopped mid-note, embarrassed that somehow I was singing out of tune. Then I heard the others, and something was definitely wrong! Their song was not right. Their melody was different and the rhythm had changed.

I looked about at the other whales and recoiled in shock. Their skin was pearly white, almost as white as mine. I blinked and then blinked again. For these were not the whales of my pod. I didn't even know if these were whales, for each one bore a twisted horn of ivory bright in the center of its head.

"Oh, tides! Am I dead or am I dreaming?" I cried. I spun round and round, trying to force my tail to my head, to feel if I somehow had grown a horn also, but to no avail.

A heavily accented voice sang to me from close range, "You are not dead and you are not dreaming, great white whale, though as a white without horn, you are an oddity, even here."

I spun to the sound, and there was another of these strange horned whales. "But what are you?" I cried.

. . . *when out of the murk of the deep*
there came two ghostly forms,
a silent bull whale and his mate.

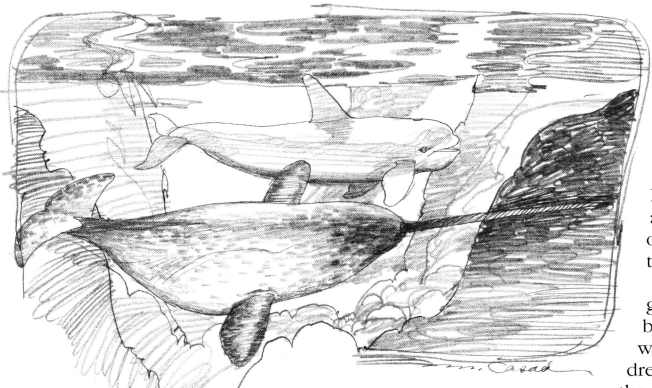

the waters of life and sang many songs as we all met together. But the sandwalkers, in fear, have spread us far about the world. Yes, there are many different songs that are being sung in the sea. But all of the songs began as one, just one song . . . our song. For our song was the beginning."

Ponderously, Mentor began toning a litany of the beginning, "As all began, the world was dryside and was drenched in the darkness of the deep. ALL THAT IS RIGHT IN THE WORLD smiled and the world was bathed in golden light."

The other Narwhal joined in explosive chorus that echoed through the ice, "This was good."

Mentor, his voice lifting and lilting in fervor, continued his chanting song, "Then, ALL THAT IS RIGHT IN THE WORLD slapped his mighty tail upon the heavens and caused the sands of the world to crash and explode, ringing smoke-filled clouds around the world."

"This was good," the other whales chanted.

"ALL THAT IS RIGHT IN THE WORLD laughed and filled the clouds with his tears of joy. Finally, he sang, allowing the skies to burst, and the rains began to fall and the world was filled and covered over with the waters of life. And in the waters of life many fishes were born. Sharp-fin, tuna-tail, and whale, all were one in the sea. And ALL THAT IS RIGHT IN THE WORLD continued his creation for a thousand tides, until the waters were filled to brimming with every form of life."

There was a pause, a beat, a measure, then all sang, "This was good."

"Are you whale or fish or something magically in-between?"

"We are the Narwhal of the Horn," sang the other whale, "and I am called Mentor. Have you never seen or heard our songs before? For others have come to hear our song. We sing of wisdom. We sing in counsel. We hold all of the melodies from all of the pods in the Song of the Sea. To us, all knowledge comes of the sandwalker and the dryside. To us comes the laughter of the porpoise and the delight of the dolphin, these snatches of song are woven into the Song of the Sea and then are sung for all to hear. For the Narwhal of the Horn were there at the beginning of it all and our song is the oldest song of all."

"I have heard of the ghosts that wander the seas, singing different melodies, but never have I seen anything of your sort," I sang in reverence.

As he chuckled, his horn bobbled in the light and a nighttime rainbow danced on his ivory staff, reflecting in bits of ice. "For you see, great white whale, the sea is filled with whales of every sort and size. Time was that whales controlled

"ALL THAT IS RIGHT IN THE WORLD looked down on all that had been created and smiled, for it was good. The smile turned to laughter, and the laughter became thunder that rolled through the darkness and golden light. Silvered tears fell from his eyes down through the skies, and the world was cleansed by the crystal waters. All the creatures of the world sang the same song and everything that was, filled the majesty of that melody.

"The waters of life surged and rolled about the world but all was not content. For there were the others, they who belonged not in the sea. The others who lolled at the surface and could not hear the song. The others who fed upon themselves in frenzy and brought discord to the song."

In a break of harmonic, the Narwhal chorus sang with angry strength, off-key and in staccato, "And that was not good."

Mentor paused and I waited, enthralled with the power of his song. Ponderously, his rich voice continued, "In its wisdom, ALL THAT IS RIGHT IN THE WORLD knew that there must be balance, and he caused the golden light to burn upon the seas and that part turned once again into cloud and the seas rolled back. Then, there was the shore, the very edge of the dryside. ALL THAT IS RIGHT IN THE WORLD listened as the song was being sung, and those that would not sing the song were cast from the waters of life and were damned to the dryside for all the tides to come—and they were called . . . sandwalkers. For then and evermore, they walked the muddy shores, longing to return to the sea and throwing stones at all of the good life they could see."

And the Narwhal in chorus sang, "Now the sea was good and right within itself."

As the horned one called Mentor continued, the song took on an ominous tone and the very rhythm changed as the other Narwhal began to softly beat the waters with their fins, "The sandwalkers were not content with all that was given

to them. They came to the edge of our world, carrying shells that would float upon the waters of life. They put their shells in the sea and stood on them, once again free to skim upon the surface of the waters of life.

"And they took from the sea but gave nothing back. In the spirit, the love of the song, we the Narwhal, went to the sandwalkers as they floated on the sea to sing to them all that must be sung. In envy, they listened. In envy, they struck a whale that sang close to their shells, killing him with their flimsy fins. When he was dead, they took his horn and used it to kill others and others. They killed all that sang, and the seas ran red with the blood of Narwhal."

The pounding on the waters became louder and louder still as they all sang, "And this was wrong. This was not good."

Mentor shook in anguish and bellowed in rage as in his mind he relived the moment, the song: "Other whales were warned of the sandwalker and they swam clear, but they who could not sing came farther and farther into the seas and killed all that could be seen. The song no longer rolled with the tides as the survivors scattered throughout the waters of life. Of the Narwhal of the Horn that survived, they swam in fear to the coldest of cold waters, in hopes they would be healed and multiply. But there were few, and they were afraid and stayed hidden in the crystal ice."

The waters rolled and tinkled hollow on the icy walls around. Silence pervaded the song and I thought that all was done, but Mentor continued and became angry, and the song, once again, took on an ominous tone.

"The sandwalkers were not content with carnage and death. To add to this insult, they cast evil things into the seas. The waters of life became sick, and all that swam close to these evil waters died or changed into hideous forms. They filled the waters with wrongness. ALL THAT IS RIGHT IN

THE WORLD began to cry bitter tears, and even this rain stung the skins of those who ventured too close to the dryside."

The song ended here, as these magical whales floated silently on a lifting wave. Mentor shook himself from his cloudy reverie and continued, "And so my little white whale, we say to you as we have said to the others that have come before us, strike back at the dryside! Strike back at the sand-walkers who kill!"

I was confused, for I didn't understand. "How can I strike at the sandwalker? I have seen them as they swim by on the shell-sharks. I have seen them kill. What possibly could I do?"

Mentor seemed pleased at my questioning, "Ah, little one, there is much you can do. As we have told others that have come, 'When a member of your pod is nearing the time of death, that time of incorporation with the waters of life, have his useless body cast upon the dryside. There it will rot and soil their air as they have soiled ours. Throw back to shore, that in part which the sand-walkers in their evil have killed. Better still, is the THOUSAND DEATHS OF THE SANDWALKER.'"

Mentor swam closer to me, until his horn was pressed to my side, and he whispered conspiratorially, "If the song of your pod is nearing completion and if one member of your pod calls out for an honorable death, then all the pod should cast themselves on the shore. All the pod should die in protest. All should die in glory of the THOUSAND DEATHS OF THE SANDWALKER. Scream your song as you die, so that the sandwalker shall know of all the evil they have cast into the waters of life."

All the Narwhal lifted the song and religiously raved, "And this shall be good!"

I trembled in thought as I realized that which he asked. "I have seen the sandwalker, and, although in part they helped in the death of my friend Adagio, I have seen no other evil you say they portend."

Mentor continued in his sing-song voice, "Go then alone as you will into the mighty waters of life and see all that you must see to believe. See all the grim reality and you then will wonder if it is real or some malformed dream. When you have seen all there is to be seen, you too will share our will. For the Narwhal waits here and speaks to the few that come seeking that which you will seek. Then, as always, they too join our quest. Soon all that sing in the sea will join our chorus. In time, all will protest the sandwalker and the cruelty he pressed on the Narwhal of the Horn."

The mists danced upon the waters as these dream whales floated, rising and falling with the gentle waves that rolled between the cliffs of ice. I thought heavily on all that had been sung, but my reverie was broken finally by the voice of Mentor.

"Your family pod now is beyond that shelf of ice." He twisted his horn and pointed to the ice looming in the distance. "Dive deep, my friend, and swim true, for a bit of your song is now part of our song." With that, they slowly floated with the tide, away into the mist.

I watched them swim in wonder, and then they faded from my view. I swam off to the shelf and again dove beneath the crystal islands of frost and rime. Once again, I breached after thinking my lungs must soon burst with fouled air that seemed to grow and expand. I looked about and saw a pod nearby. I listened and was delighted to hear Cacophony's groans and burps as he railed at me, "Where have you been, kelp-breath?"

Ignoring his salty remarks, I hurriedly sought Tympani. Once I found him, I sang quickly of the Narwhal of the Horn, and only when I was finished did I realize that others of the pod had gathered to listen to my song.

"Tsk, tsk," they sang. "Harmony must have bumped his head on the ice, for Narwhal of the Horn are what dreams and ghosts are made of." Clucking a gentle song of sympathy, they swam

Everywhere I looked were reflections of me.
Like an echo of light,
many Harmonies bounced and glittered all around me.

away, leaving me alone with the aging whale called Philosophy, and Tympani, the scribe.

"The others don't believe me!" I cried out in total frustration.

Philosophy mused aloud as he, too, began swimming away, "His song is odd but it is great with food for thought."

"Not to worry, Harmony," consoled Tympani. "For whether or not the Narwhal of the Horn were real or dream is unimportant, for the beauty was still yours to see. As to the journey they asked you to take, the decision is yours. Others before you have swum alone for a time to see what they must see, but when finished with your journey you must return, so I can add your travels to our Song of the Sea." With that, he, too, swam away, leaving me alone with my disquieted thoughts, as the northern colored lights danced upon the sky.

I did nothing but exist for several tides after my meeting with the Narwhal. All of the younger whales teased me, calling me "the dream whale," and would burst into bubbles of laughter if I swam deep with them. All of this I ignored, preferring to wrestle with the reality or the lack of reality in what I had seen. Most of all, I questioned whether I had met them at all.

I labored hard, and there were times that I felt I would never know the answers to my questioning. That did not stop me from having my favorite friend, Melody, examine my head for any sign of concussion or contusion. Other than tickling me to near distraction, she found nothing.

Were they real or had I dreamed them? Very little captured my attention then, so unmindful was I by what had or had not happened. Once again I sought out the wisdom of Tympani.

It took me most of a tide to find him, for he was on the other side of the pod and I was avoiding Cacophony who was in very foul spirits. Nothing

would cheer him more than to beat upon me. I found Tympani in the late afternoon recording a new passage to the song and I waited patiently and silently at his tail, as was the tradition. When he finished, he turned to me and said, "I had a feeling that you would seek me out."

I wondered how Tympani could possibly "have a feeling" about what I was going to do when I didn't know myself. Regardless, I struggled on. "I ponder this question of the Narwhal: Were they real? Is there a place in our song that talks of the horned ones?"

Tympani paused and I am sure his mind raced through melody after melody searching for all reference to my question. Finally, after some time, he spoke, "Yes, my Harmony, there is reference to the Narwhal. It is true they were there at the beginning when ALL THAT IS RIGHT IN THE WORLD created the sea and the song. It is true there is reference, though very vague, as to the THOUSAND DEATHS OF THE SANDWALKER. It became part of our song from the ghosting songs of another pod. Therefore, it is not strong and may have been twisted by the currents that flow."

"But," I repeated, "is it true? Are they real? Did I have this experience or was it indeed some kind of delusion?"

This wise, gentle whale mused a bit and then sang again, "Whether it was delusion, dream, or reality matters not. Sometimes reality appears dreamlike and unreal. Sometimes dreams appear as reality. But one can learn from both, and both are equally important."

That statement spun my mind round. Dreams that were reality. Reality that was dream. Possibly Tympani had eaten a soft fish that caused him to hallucinate. I shook his thoughts from my head and persisted. "Are the Narwhal real?"

"Harmony," he patiently continued, "all that you sang was true. The Narwhal were among the

in these cold waters by the crystal goodness of the sun.

"Mother, I have decided to travel. I am to seek answers to questions that fill my mind with confusion. I wish to carry your blessing, a bit of your song, with me as a charm to protect from the new and the sometimes frightening."

Her beautiful eyes blinked as she looked at me in her gentle way. I had thought, perhaps hoped, that she would try to dissuade me, to convince me that all was folly, but I was to be disappointed. "Harmony, my son, you must always seek the truth in that which surrounds you, and if truth is not there, then seek it out wherever it may be. Carry this bit of song and be not gone too long, for I love you."

I slid my body near to her, touching that which was a part of me. We swam tandem, side-by-side until we were both assured, and then I departed, sadness in my wake. I sought Melody and when I found her, I excitedly told her of my decision to go alone into the seas and search. The other young whales gathered around, eyes wide in the excitement of my journey.

My enthusiastic ramblings were interrupted soon enough by the belchings of Cacophony as he bulled his way through the other whales to where I swam with Melody. "Well, bubble breath, what's this I hear about your leaving?"

I repeated the intent of my journey. I was shocked that Cacophony didn't immediately sing that it was stupid. He floated beside, studying me slowly with those careful predator eyes of his. He said nothing for a moment or two as our eyes

first of the whales. They chose to make contact with the early sandwalkers that did for the second time venture into the sea. But it is sung in the song that they were all killed. None of them lived. They are no more, forever. They are thought of only as THEY WHO WERE."

I left in a daze and floated alone far to the side of the pod, more questions having been created than answered.

Then, after some time, with a flip of my tail I shook off my lethargy and resolutely swam to my mother, Rhapsody, whom I had not seen in many tides. She was swimming in the midst of the great pod, skimming the surface, warmed coldly locked. He and I were always in combat. This time, though, he saw my resolve, and he blinked first. Embarrassed, he slapped me with his mighty fluke and laughingly said, "Well, good luck, fish bait. You'll need it. Someday I will eat of your flesh second hand in the belly of a large sharp-fin." With a massive splash, he dove and was gone.

I turned my thoughts once again to Melody, "Well, I guess I had better go," I said, stumbling for the right thing to say and the right way to say it. Unfortunately, my hopes for a poetic goodbye were dashed as a swell lifted our two bodies together in a sensual way. Flustered, I muttered, "Uh, eat lots of fish."

She also was awkward, and sang in her sweet voice, "You too."

With that immortal farewell, I swam away from the pod and out to sea. The song surrounded me for some time, but little by little, it faded until it was nothing more than a gentle echo and then, it was gone. My ears rang with the silence as I swam alone in the great sea. It is odd how alone you really feel when you leave that which you have become so accustomed to. Big becomes bigger.

I swam, feeding as the need arose, for the seas were rich and I exalted in the adventure. I swam through two tides and far into another before I realized I didn't know where I was going. I was seeking truth. I was seeking to find the sandwalker to verify or vilify the truth of the Narwhal. But where were the sandwalkers? I finally decided the best course was to swim nearer to the dryside, where I would find answers.

I swam through light and dark, and dark and light, until my eyes blurred with exhaustion. Finally, on the twelfth tide, I found a shell-shark, the bearer of sandwalkers, or rather it nearly found me. I had just breached from the deep after feeding and was allowing the sun to soak warmth into my body, when from behind, a squeaky voice laughed out in sing-song fashion, "Out of the way. Out of the way. Sandwalkers come looking for fun and they can't seem to find their way."

I spun quickly in the water, and there was a shell-shark bearing down, white froth pushing at its nose. I sank into the safety of the deep, my heart pounding in my ears. "Where was the warning—the hum, the song that is not a song— that flows with every shell-shark I have seen?" I questioned myself out loud.

I was rattled to my very soul when the squeaky voice answered, "This shell-shark is silent. It follows the wind." I looked for the source of the voice and was shocked to see a small whale-like creature before me. Bigger than a tuna-tail, smaller than the large sharp-fins, it floated like a dream, squeaking its silly songs.

"What are you?" I asked. "You nearly sing the whale song, but you are not whale. What are you?"

"Hmmm," it gigglingly sang, "What are I? Well, I are not sandwalker. I are not whale. If I are not these things, then I must be dolphin." With that, he quickly swam towards me and stopped just inches from my eyes. "My name is Little Brother. And that," he said turning, indicating yet another dolphin swimming quickly towards us, "is my mate, Laughter Ring. Our duty as dolphins is to lead the way before yonder shell-shark."

"But why?" I asked.

"Why? You, of all creatures, ask, 'Why?'" he laughed. "Because if we didn't lead the way, yonder shell-shark would run over dumb whales like you. Besides, the sandwalkers that ride the shell-shark make us laugh and dolphins live to laugh."

My back humped. "I have never been thought of as dumb, Little Brother," I grumbled angrily. "Best watch who you speak to so flippantly." "Flippantly?" he laughed. "Flippantly? If you wish, great whale, I shall flippantly flick my flipping flappers and fly." He slipped beneath the

I spun quickly in the water,
and there was a shell-shark bearing down,
white froth pushing at its nose.

waters and then leaped across my back not once, not twice, but thrice. I was becoming very angry, and the thought crossed my mind of whether or not this dolphin would make a filling meal.

"He means not harm," giggled Laughter Ring, his mate, as she glided to where we floated. "He means only to make you smile and laugh at all the fun that spreads beneath the sun."

I calmed myself. After all, I had been called much worse by Cacophony. Slowly, together my strange companions and I rose to the surface and breached onto the gently rolling sea.

With my composure regained, I looked at the dolphins and asked, "You say that the sand-walkers make you laugh. How can that be? I have seen the sandwalkers in their shell-sharks before, and in their wake I have only found death and destruction."

"Oh, 'tis true," spoke Little Brother as he again took over the dialog. "Most of the sandwalkers are evil to their very core, but some are fun, and many, in their simple way, bring joy to me on a sunny day. Look, even as we sing, they turn their lumbering shell to follow us."

I looked, and as Little Brother had said, the shell-shark was turning and heading our way. I started to dive deep but was stopped by the dolphin, "Fear not, my friend. They will not hurt you. They are curious and love to touch all they see."

I was horrified, "You would allow them to touch you?"

"Yup," said he, "It doesn't hurt, and besides, it tickles."

Not to be outdone by a tiny dolphin, but with much trepidation, I lay still in the water and waited and watched. After all, I was on this journey to seek the truth, and the truth in part was sailing my way. If I died, so be it. I watched in morbid fascination as the shell-shark drew near. This was the likes of a shell-shark that I had never seen before, the same, yet different. For this shell had white kelp-like clouds hung high above. As I watched, I could see for the first time sandwalkers scurrying like crabs about the shell to draw the kelp clouds down.

The shell slid quietly to us and I waited expectantly. The dolphins began cavorting in the water, dancing on their tails and the like. After a time, they tired of this and swam back to me. "The sandwalkers care not for us today. They are more entertained to look at you, great white whale. Go to them; feel their strange dry skin upon your flesh."

Challenged by this pip-squeak of a dolphin, I nervously moved close to the shell and cast my eye upon the creatures above. They were strange looking, with sea grass waving on their heads. Their fins were thin and their bodies were covered in odd-colored scales.

I waited, rolling in the surf, not knowing whether I would be tickled or stabbed with a mighty horn of the Narwhal. Fortunately, one of the sandwalkers reached a flimsy fin down and touched my side above my eye. I blinked in fear, but nothing happened. If anything, there was a gentleness about the stroking. I listened and could barely hear these strange creatures almost singing to themselves. "Maybe they too have a song," I sang, "but it is an odd song without depth. Possibly, if I took them to the deep, they would be able to sing with more strength."

Little Brother and Laughter Ring rolled in the sea, bathing me in gales of laughter. "I think not, my friend. They know not how to hold their breath."

We stayed beside the shell for a great time as I saw all that I could see, and finally I called to my new friends, "I must leave. For this is perplexing. I have been told by the Narwhal in dream that the sandwalker brings death to the sea. Now I find that they are not so bad and I must go back to my pod and add this to our Song of the Sea."

I turned to go but was stopped by the dolphins. "Ah," said Laughter Ring, "all the sandwalkers are not as these. Some—and most—do bring death."

"Then," I continued, "I must seek them out, wherever they may be. For I have many answers given to me by the Narwhal that have need of questions to be asked."

"Well," laughed the dolphin, "we shall guide you if you will have us. For we have traveled far and we have seen what you seek." With a flip of their tails, they were off in a flash even before I

could answer. I turned once and looked back at the shell-shark and the sandwalkers it bore. It was odd, but as I swam away one of the creatures waved a fin, almost as if to say goodbye. Maybe they do carry a song.

With this thought to carry me on my journey, I strongly surged after my newly acquired guides to the sea and new songs to be sung.

We swam, my friends and I, on and on. Our direction was upward to the cold pure waters of summer. As we traveled, I listened intently for other whale songs, but there were none. I listened also for the shell-sharks but our trip was uneventful. The dolphins kept up a running commentary on all they saw—now, saw before, and possibly might see in the future. Everything was filled with laughter to the dolphins. Drifting bits of dryside stick, glops of kelp following the current, all was a source of mirth and merriment. They laughed at me. They laughed at life as it swam by. They even laughed at themselves.

Laughter Ring was the quieter of the two, but, like her name, her laughter would ring about the sea as Little Brother came floating by with a crown of seaweed or mush-fish on his head. I have never laughed so much in my life. You would think, as did I, that after a time the humor would grow old, but they were as adept at laughter as the whale was of song, and I never grew tired of laughing with them.

I had first counted the tides as they moved with the dark of the silverside, but as I reached one hundred I stopped counting. Tide after tide, we swam. Until one and all were exhausted of our journey but not of our company. Later, when the sea was very cold and the skies were filled with snow, I asked Little Brother when I would see that which I should see. For the first time ever, he became somber and resolute.

"There is a taste in the water," said he, as he shuddered in revulsion, "of the sandwalker and the evil he brings to the sea. Come next tide, two at the most, you will see that which you won't want to see."

We swam slower now and the sea was filled with floating massive chunks of crystal water. Early the following tide, we came upon a great group of flipper-fins. Delighted was I at this change of menu, and I dove quickly in chase of a large tasty meal. He was a wild one, that flipper-fin, but I had become an experienced hunter. Filled with the savory meat, I surfaced near my friends who looked at me in total shock.

"What is the matter?" I sang, "Is there some evil in the water, some sandwalker drawing near?"

Laughter Ring wouldn't even talk, so disgusted was she, but Little Brother spoke angrily, "You speak of seeking the sandwalker and wish to see their evil ways. Yet, you prey on and eat the flesh of our near-to-cousins, the flipper-fins."

I was startled. Many times the pod had feasted on flipper-fins and I was taught in their ways. "That's impossible; I've never heard them sing."

"You and your bloody songs," Laughter Ring snapped. "Not all are related by a musical song alone. Listen as they speak in the water. Listen to their words so true as they dash in fear of the brutal you!"

Her anger lashed me, much worse than any beating at the fins of Cacophony. I listened, as she had asked, but heard nothing but the fearful barkings of flipper-fin. "I hear not but the bark," I said frustrated.

"That," said Little Brother, "is the song of the flipper-fin. Whether you know it or not, they are of our family and yours."

The meal once so warm and secure in my belly began to roll queasily. I listened again and I could hear the crude beginnings of song in the now-speech of the flipper-fin. They sang of fear. They sang of the great white hunter who killed their leader. They sang, warning all in the sea to leap to the frozen islands to escape the fiend.

It took me a bit of time to realize that I was the great white hunter . . . I was the fiend. Sickened now, I moved away and became very ill for a time. Later, I know not how long, I moved silently back to my friends shamefacedly. They spoke not a word as we quietly moved through the icy waters, but I knew what they were thinking.

After a time, Laughter Ring whispered quietly, "Keep low in the water and watch the shore of the dryside. There you will see part of that which you seek."

I looked to the shore and watched the flipper-fins that cavorted there, safe from the menace in the sea. In time, there came a movement, and I sighted sandwalkers moving swiftly along on spindly fins against the water's edge, as if to pen the flipper-fins farther from the sea. They moved with deliberation and purpose. The large male flipper-fins were allowed to escape into the water, but the females and the babies were left to their own devices, and the sandwalkers were intent that they shouldn't escape.

As my eyes stared in blinkless disbelief, these evil creatures, these sandwalkers, swung dryside sticks and beat the babies to death. The cries of the young dying mixed with the painful agony as parents watched their children die.

I turned shaken and spoke to my guides, "The sandwalker gathers meat, as does the pod. They are no better or worse than the whale."

"Look again, dear friend," cried Little Brother as tears traced down his silver skin. "They are much worse than you, who seek a meal."

I gazed again at the shore and was shocked to see the sandwalkers ripping the furry skin off the dead children and tossing the carcass away. Over and over, this was repeated until hundreds of babies were dead and discarded. Then, as quickly

. . . the babies were left to their own devices,
and the sandwalkers were intent they shouldn't escape.

as they had come, the sandwalkers left the blood-red beach to the crying mothers and the very few young ones who had survived.

Unable to help and unable to watch or listen anymore, we moved out to sea to cleanse the filth from our eyes and ears. "I should have snapped the arm from the sandwalker on the shell that touched me before it could do this harm," I growled angrily, not even able to sing in song.

"It wasn't them," said Laughter Ring very subdued. "For there are many sandwalkers. Some are good, but some are bad."

We rolled in the sea, soothed by the silence. At last, I roused myself from my introspection and said, "Now, I must return to the pod. For I have seen the good and the evil of the sandwalker and there are many lessons that must be sung into the song."

I assumed my friends would be delighted to be rid of their cannibalistic guest, but Laughter Ring spoke again, "Not yet, my great white. There is more that you should see."

"More," I cried. "More of the sandwalkers killing the flipper-fin young and then defying the basest law of the sea by not consuming their kill?"

"No," answered Little Brother, "it is worse than that. Much, much worse."

My heart hammered in my throat as I followed my two now-quiet guides. I knew not if they were silent and remorseful because of my actions earlier or if it was the death of the flipper-fins. No matter, I didn't feel like laughter, and the silence was a golden balm to soothe the pain of watching that which we had watched. We ate sparingly of the bottom fish, bug-eye, and flat-tail and sped quickly down from the cold, following the swift currents that moved us on our journey.

Little Brother and Laughter Ring frolicked occasionally to bring a wry smile to my face. For the most part, we swam hard, and there wasn't time for talk, let alone laughter. The water changed as the air warmed and there seemed to be a smell or a taste, I knew not which, which had wrongness about it. Often, we would have to swim around or deep under a floating island of rot and filth. Objects, the likes of which I had never seen, floated crazily on the water, but they smelled of evil and close inspection was not advised.

Little Brother explained that all of these objects and all of this filth was from the sandwalkers that lived on the dryside nearby. The water was so fouled that my skin began to turn an oily black. Laughter Ring said that I had begun to look like a real whale, but I was not amused at the transformation.

We swam very close to the dryside and there was a strange death all around. Fishes had been changed and malformed by some devious magic of the sandwalkers. We pushed on and finally, in the distance, we could hear the plaintive cries of other dolphins. Tired though we were, we swam faster and closed in on their pleas for help.

What we found was hideous beyond belief. Dolphins wrapped in kelp-like streamers that held them fast. Some were dead; others were dying. The sea was filled with the screams of torture as the dolphins tried desperately to rip free from their death-bound prison. Without fear of consequence, I tore at this net of death with my teeth, but only one was freed. I tried and tried again, unable to bear the screams of pain and anguish.

I was finally pushed firmly away by Little Brother and Laughter Ring. "Try not, our friend," they cried, "for these dolphins have been trapped too long. If they lived, they would be stranger still, for they have been long without the sweet air to fill their lungs."

I backed away, watching in horror as tens, maybe hundreds, of dolphins died in that cove. Above, we could see the sandwalkers milling about their shells doing nothing. Soon the sandwalkers began to pull their kelp-like material to the surface, and the dolphins that were found there, still clinging to life, were beaten until the water ran red. Once killed, they were thrown with the fishes up into the shells of the sandwalker . . . an ignominious death.

When all was done and silence returned to the sea, I asked, "Why? The fishes are food for all to share as was commanded by ALL THAT IS RIGHT IN THE WORLD, but the dolphins have song. Why do they die?"

"We don't know," answered the two dolphins sadly.

Little brother continued, "We think that the sandwalkers believe all the fishes to be theirs. We think that they don't wish to share, and kill anything that gets in the way. But we really don't know why. We, the dolphins, love all things created, even the wandwalker, but we are rewarded at times like these with death."

"I have seen enough!" I anguished. "Now surely you will let me return to my pod to add all these horrors to the song. To tell of the right and to tell of the wrong."

"No!" shouted Laughter Ring. "There is one more that you should see. You must know all if you seek the truth."

Knowing my pain at seeing all this for the first time, Little Brother tried to console me, "It isn't far, and it truly is on your way back to your pod."

I was so numbed by all I had seen that I meekly followed as they led me back to the sea and the sweetness of the open water. We swam slowly, in

silence. I, for one, had nothing to say and much to think upon—and much more that I wish I could forget.

But the worst was yet to come. As we swam true to the rising golden light, the water seemed to reverberate with keening, a soft, high-pitched sound. We swam hard, and the noise increased until we were bathed in its unearthly song.

Suddenly, Little Brother and Laughter Ring stopped. "Go no closer, my friend, but see what you can see from where we are."

I looked and saw on the horizon many shell-sharks that must be filled with hundreds of sandwalkers, so large were they. "I must go closer. I can barely see," I protested.

"You don't understand," choked Laughter Ring. "You are in mortal danger here. For the sandwalkers kill not flipper-fin or dolphins. Here, they kill the song itself."

I shook my head still not totally understanding.

Little Brother came close to my side and whispered, "Here, they kill the song. Here, they murder the whale. All that swim with this pod will die."

Against their warning, I blindly surged forward. It wasn't long before the water turned brown with the blood-sludge of death. I looked about and watched as strange screaming shell-sharks, not unlike the ones that had mortally wounded Adagio, chased whale after whale and stabbed them deep with an object which I presumed was a Narwhal horn. Keening pervaded the water, but it was not the screaming shells. It was the wordless hum of death from the whales.

Amidst all this carnage, a small yellow shell-shark raced madly about with a single sandwalker standing inside. I watched, thinking of ways to attack the little one and wreak some small form of vengeance. But then I noticed something odd, this little yellow shell was turning the bigger shells aside. With each one turned aside, a whale was saved and was able to dive to the deep.

I watched as the little shell raced towards me and I steeled for an attack, but the shell raced on by. As I turned, I saw that it was diverting yet another shell-shark that was about to attack me. When the bigger shell-shark backed away, the smaller shell raced by me again on the way to help another whale. As it raced by, the sandwalker raised his puny fin and waved, like the one so long ago, as if to say goodbye.

Laughter Ring and Little Brother guided me away, into empty waters. I dove deep and allowed the mighty pressure of ALL THAT IS RIGHT IN THE WORLD to cleanse my soul. I sang of the song that had died, and I sang for the souls of the whales that had gone to the end . . . the beginning.

Finally, when all the sweetness of life was gone from my lungs, I surfaced where my friends waited for me patiently. "I don't know whether to love you for showing me all this or hate you forever. My song is filled with confusion," I sang.

"Go now to your pod," they sang in gentle voices. "Though you be confused, remember that there is good and bad in all things. You must learn to value each for its balance. Someday we will meet again and share a memory and we will learn to laugh again." And with that they disappeared.

Filled with emptiness, I began the slow journey back to the safety of my pod, yearning for the comfort of my own kind. I had journeyed a long, long time; there was much to sing to the song.

EXPOSITION

I wasted no time on the journey home to the pod. I stopped rarely to eat and never to sleep. Many times I had to force myself to snag a fish just to maintain my strength. What I had experienced reeled through my mind like a song sung off-key.

There was much to think about. Some of the sandwalkers were evil. Many of the sandwalkers were good. All of them tried to sing, albeit though a tiny snatch of song.

The protest as proclaimed and advocated by the Narwhal was true in its intent, but was more death the answer? Should we answer the death of our brothers and cousins with sacrificial death? Was there not some better way? Was there not an answer to this dying in the seas besides the THOUSAND DEATHS OF THE SANDWALKER? The sandwalker was truly paradox, for there were many good but seemed to be many more evil. Surely ALL THAT IS RIGHT IN THE WORLD must have some reason for allowing all this to continue. These thoughts and others like them raced through my mind like a sharp-fin in feeding frenzy.

As I swam, I listened for traces of the pod's song, and though I heard other bits of melody, the tunes did not run true. Finally, some fifteen hundred tides after I had left as a capricious youth, I returned an older, wiser, and much subdued whale. It was odd fate, as I neared the coast of the dryside, that the first I heard of the song was Cacophony telling all that he would feed first, and whatever was left as scraps, they could feed upon.

I sang briefly announcing my return, and, of course, the first to meet me was the mad bull himself. As I approached, he stopped still in the water, his massive body having grown during my travels.

His voice had not improved with age. He sang to me in his arrogant way, "Well, well, if it isn't the wayfaring stranger himself. It's too bad you weren't eaten."

"Best understand, bubble-breath," he continued, "that I control this pod. Soon, when my father has the sense to flip over dead, I will be the scribe. Then I will sing the song, and you will have to listen."

I was tired, hungry, and in no spirit to listen to any of his railing. "Back off!" I rumbled. "Go beat on a jelly fish, for that is your style." With that, I brushed by him. He probably would have thrashed me then and there, so weak was I, but my tone was assured; and being the bully he was, he only attacked when he was sure he would win.

I moved through the mass of the pod and swam directly to Tympani, who was accompanied by the old philosopher, Philosophy. A hush fell over the pod, and it seemed to me that even the seas were smoothed. In a strong but tired voice, I sang my song as I had heard it sung. The pod was quiet still as I finished. No one moved, and the wind fell flat.

Philosophy was the first to break the silence as he idly floated away musing, "Much food for thought. Much thought is needed."

Tympani sang soothingly, "You have done well by the song, my young friend, but now you

must rest and build your strength. When you are fulfilled, come to me and we will sing more your adventures."

Rest I did. I filled my body with the sweet meats that ran free in the sea, but never again did I touch the meat of the flipper-fin. I remained alone in self-imposed isolation, wrestling with all. The answers that I sought had to be in the song. I vowed to learn all I could from Tympani before his death and the passing of that song to his son, Cacophony.

Once rested, I spent all my free time consumed with the Song of the Sea. Always near Tympani, as many tides passed, I listened to the song unfold. I listened and repeated the song with the other whales, as Tympani sang all that needed to be sung.

One silver tide of darkside, Tympani stopped in the water as if listening to some unsung melody. "It is time," he sang to the pod. "It is my time. I have lived a long, wonderful life. But now I am old and it is time for the waters of life to wash over me no more."

I listened in silent shock as this great, quiet whale portended his own death, his own end, his beginning. My silence did not go unnoticed, for Tympani sang a gentle tune to me, "Birth and death are nearly the same: the end and the beginning. My time is marked upon the sea and I have nothing to fear in giving myself back to the waters of life. The loss will be felt by you and the others, but that is the melody of the song for as long as it is sung. I will be remembered, and in the music of the memory, there is no end, no death."

By this time, the rest of the pod had gathered around the aging scribe of the Song of the Sea. He sang loudly so all could hear and none would forget, "Tradition calls for me in dying to pass the song on to the new scribe—a new recorder—my son, Cacophony. But traditions are created by those they serve, so I will change that which has been for all of the tides in the sea. Rather than passing the song on to my son, Cacophony, I will pass the song to Harmony, the great white, so that the song will be sung for all eternity."

The seas moved in silence and no one of the pod moved with the echoes of the music that was sung. Finally, at the back of the pod, a great thrashing and wailing began as the news rested with Cacophony. "It was mine . . . the song was mine to sing as scribe. May you all be carved by the sandwalkers. This is bilge and flotsam!" With that he noisily crashed deep into the water, his vile curses soiling the sea.

I was honored. I was thrilled. But I was saddened more by the loss of my dear friend.

Tympani solemnly continued, "Come dive with me, my Harmony. There in the deepest of deep and the cleanest of waters, I will sing the Song of the Sea for you to record and remember for your lifetime."

With that, the aging whale breached and dove deep into the sea. I looked at my mother and my friends knowing that when I returned all would be changed forever. But the song called to me and I listened.

I dropped into the sea. Deeper than deep I fell in spiral, following the haunting melody of the past and the future to be. Down and down, round and round into the coldest, blackest water. There in the emerald dark of the sea, I found the shadowed form of my dear, dying friend Tympani, the scribe.

As the pressure settled about me like a well-worn mantle, Tympani began to sing the Song of the Sea, "The pod was born in a flash of light that was the beginning and the end of all things. We were there at the edge of creation and will be there when creation crumbles." His voice, like the tides rushing through crystal coral, rang true and I listened and remembered all. He sang songs of the sandwalkers and their crude entrance to the dryside, of their foaming desire to rid the seas of all that sing. He sang of the destruction and of the death, the crying and dying as songs were stopped before they were sung.

He sang of births and beginnings and of the glorious passing of the song from one scribe to another, over millions and millions of tides. He sang of the structure of the pod, the conductors who lead and must be followed if there is to be a melody. He sang of the composers, the creators that force new melodies upon the pod. He sang of rhythm and rhyme.

He sang loudly the praises of Philosophy, our dreamer, and now the oldest living member of the pod . . . Philosophy, who dared to dream of things undreamed, and who shared with all the pod his thoughts of the deep and its relationship with the dryside and those creatures beyond.

Tympani sang as I had never heard him sing of all things before—even the birth of me, the great white Harmony, destined to grandeur by the oddity of being born. When he sang of Adagio, a tear came to my eye as I remembered the innocence of youth and the striking force of growing older.

Finally he sang to me the responsibility of the scribe and all that he must do, the sacrifices that must be made in order to save the song at all cost. "A scribe must never be directly involved in any action, but rather, must stand aside and record the events as they happen. He must listen to the glorious melodies of birth and death. He must listen to the laughter without laughing, the sadness without shedding a tear. For no matter what the pattern or melody, the Scribe must stand to the side and record and remember the Song of the Sea. If the pod should cease to be, the Scribe must pass this song to another pod and thus insure the continuance of eternity."

He paused as the song ended and then sang only for me, "You are so young, my dear great white Harmony," he sang, "but the whole of the melody is now part and parcel with your spirit. You are now the scribe and I, at last, am free. Come with me and listen, as I sing my final song and suffer, yet exalt, in the glory of the end, the beginning, the incorporation with the waters of life." With that, he sank deeper still into the heavier waters and began to hum a haunting melody, the melody of death and dying.

The song had taught me that the passing was a time of celebration of oneness with all that is, but I could not help but be gripped by sadness. As I listened and remembered all that I saw of Tympani's quiet passing, I felt a loss I had not felt before, a regret at not knowing him better, regret at not seeing all that he saw when he saw it.

Tympani's hums were quiet and gentle as he chose to die in silence and reflection. His reverie, however, was shockingly interrupted by a flash of slick-black flesh as Tympani was rolled and rammed by another whale . . . Cacophony!

The gentle hums became strained and discordant as Cacophony rammed his father over and over screaming, "Want to die the quiet death, old man? Want to end your tides in dignity? Then give me the Song of the Sea." As if in answer, Tympani stopped all singing and accepted the brutal abuse in silence, which only enraged and angered the bull to attack again and again.

With mighty flips of my flukes, I surged to rescue my old friend. I was nearly in the middle of the melee when Tympani with his last strength sang out, "No! Harmony, stand off! You are the scribe, never to be involved, never to interfere. You, as the singer of the song, must watch and wait. Do nothing. It is my wish and the command of the song."

"Yes, singer, listen," roared Cacophony, "I will give you a song to sing." With that he smashed his massive head again into the side of Tympani. But Tympani did not cry out, and the water slowly

There in the emerald dark of the sea,
I found the shadowed form
of my dear, dying friend Tympani, the scribe . . .

filled with gentle harmonic humming as a smile crossed the old whale's face like the shadow of sun and cloud on the sea. With that, Tympani passed into the end . . . the beginning.

Cacophony continued to ram repeatedly the now-vacant flesh but finally realized that his torment was in vain. He stood back confused. Then, in a flash of tail and fluke, he was gone. I floated nearby remembering all there was to remember of the song. For the song was now everything and all. In respect to the memory of his father, I didn't chase after Cacophony and ram him into the deep. Instead, I surfaced and, with all the strength in me, sang the new verse of the Song of the Sea to all that would listen of the ignominious death of the greatest scribe of all, Tympani.

Anger was the wound, and time was the healer. But as the now singer of the song, the scribe, I was damned to remember—forever.

As night turned to day, turned to night, like the flickering of one's eye, I found myself distancing from the pod as I learned to listen. Circling, always circling, listening for all the new gentle melodies. With the listening came learning, and knowledge filled the empty voids of loneliness. As time and tides passed, innocence washed from me, and my senses became dulled. My sensitivity became objectivity as I concentrated on the song—only the song. It coursed through my veins, chilling my blood until no day passed when I didn't feel a bit colder and very numb.

As we swam from cold to warm to stormy seas and back again, my peers, the others of my age and birthing all seemed younger and different, yet paradoxically the same. I could sing of them and all their adventures but I never joined with them again.

I watched and recorded the joys that occurred and also the anguish and heartache. A worse fate was that I was forced to watch, remember and sing of Cacophony's railings and of his discordant belches of life. Listening to him sing was like listening to a rock sing to the sand, but as was my charge, I listened and recorded, making all a part of the song.

Cacophony did not run alone. Slowly, as the tides changed, some of the whales began to follow his strength whether right or wrong. One of these was a whale called Metronome, who never could decide whether he was whale or jellyfish and life was a game of pretending. What he never pretended, though, was deep and undying love for Cacophony's strength. He drank of it, and slowly he lost his own personality, becoming a shadow to the hulk of the discordant whale.

Cacophony used Metronome as a game piece, an object of interference when needed. When Cacophony was caught in his net of lies and cowardice, he would simply say, "Metronome did it!" and this simple fish accepted these accusations from his blocker of light, as a compliment and acceptance. His moony eyes would widen in pride whenever Cacophony called his name—for whatever reason.

It was at this time that all the younger whales passed from the warm waters of youth to the colder chill of adulthood. This fact was strange to watch and record as a part and parcel of the song. Like the blinded lustful salmon that rushed from the sea to the waters-lacking-salt for procreation, the young of the pod, those born with me and some much later, blindly ignored the brightness of the light that danced on the waters. They missed much because of their eagerness to dive to the deep where they would be called adult, take a mate, bear young, grow old and die.

They taught themselves to squint in the sun and limit their vision, and in this act somehow came the wonderfulness of adulthood, but much was missed. As they rushed with the current of time, their dreams began to die and with that death so went the laughter of innocence. With the death of the dreams came the inability to hear clearly the Song of the Sea and the great variety of melodies that lay within.

Even I was attracted to the deep and I teased myself with its feeling of strength and pressure. Though I often thought of taking a mate and could feel my blood warm to life's current, the responsibilities of my life as the scribe brought me back to my senses. To watch objectively from a distance was almost to freeze time in place, though I never forgot how to dream. But the dreams were nearly shattered one day as I recorded a bit of song that was sung very off-key.

Cacophony had already taken a mate, a silly cow by the name of Percussion. Her name was apt, for her singing was as the beating of a weed on a water-soaked log. She was in the constant want of Cacophony, a fact he both relished and ignored.

As Percussion became slow and great with the calf that grew inside, Cacophony's eye wandered to the other mateless whales. One of these was my friend, Melody, who always sang to me dear gentle tunes of laughter breaking like frothing waves on the sea. She often sang of the moonlight dancing on the waters and, of her, I would drink deep and remember forever. Cacophony wanted her as much for her song, as for the fact that she sang to me.

Then one bright silverside, Cacophony and his shadowy, off-beat friend, Metronome, cornered Melody in a smooth-watered cove close to shore. "Well, well, well," crowed Cacophony in his discordant

rumbling tones, "look here, Metronome, we have a delectable bit of fish. Sweet and tightly meated. Melody, let's you and I join together as one to taste those saltless waters!"

Melody swam deeper into the cove. As she sought escape from eminent disaster, she taunted him to gain time, "Oh, but Cacophony you have sung the song that only can be sung to one, to Percussion who bears your young. Are you to violate all the laws and mate with two or three? For, if this is true, then why not mate with your shadow, Metronome? Though he be male, it is sung that he can sing a two-part harmony." With that, she dove deep, trying to dive beneath Cacophony. But the bull was fast, and with

mighty kicks of his flukes, he dove and blocked her escape from the cove.

Cacophony's eyes flashed wild, sparked with anger like clashing rocks on a wind-torn shore. "Don't you fool with me, Melody. The pod knows that you yearn to mate with Harmony, the great white. But we all know that he is made impotent by the song that he must carry."

Melody turned to retreat back into the cove,

but her way was blocked by Metronome, who had quietly followed her. "Are you going somewhere, my gentle squid?" he called. "My master wishes you to stay."

She began to swim in ever-tighter circles as the two hedged closer. The great bull bellowed a rankling tune. "Harmony, great white, where are you? Where is the scribe when you need him to record an important passage in the song? Harmony, come record this song as I mate with this sweet-meated tuna. For I am Cacophony! I am destined by the blood that boils in my loins to father my own pod."

As was my responsibility, I stood off near the breakers of this coral sea and listened to the song as it was poorly sung. But the song broke down by the waves that pounded at my head, and I could listen no more. Filled with the haunting melodies of Adagio and Tympani as they had died from the result of this throw-back, I charged. Borne by the strength of the tide at my back, I smashed into Cacophony's side. Bubbles blew, and the sweet air that maintains life was forced from the massive bull. He breached, gasped, and then dove in the blinding anger that was his special kind.

"Ahh, the scribe has feelings yet," he rumbled. "How dare you to attack the greatest whale ever! Come fight me, scribe. I am yet to have the Song of the Sea."

Anger replaced reason. As he dove, I twisted on my spine and, with all the strength I could muster, smashed my head into his side as he overshot his mark. Stunned, he floated between sunlight and the waters deep. I attacked again and again.

"Are you going somewhere, my gentle squid?"
he called. "My master wishes you to stay."

How many times I do not remember.
I could hear and see nothing but the death of this whale. I hammered and slashed, and for the first time in my life, I wouldn't sing the song.

I backed Cacophony to the shore and prepared to end his life, once and for all. But the way was blocked by whale. At first, I thought it was Metronome, but as I regained my senses, I could hear him keening a song of fear and loathing far out to sea. The whale before me was older than old. His skin was dulled by many tides and hung slack like waters without waves.

His voice, querulous, yet rang with authority. "Scribe, stop that which you do! Death as you wish it for Cacophony is wrong, but that does not make him right. Leave him be! For you are now the wrongness in the sea. You have violated the mightiest melody of the song. You are scribe, and scribe is commanded by all that is holy never to interfere. Scribe is charged with standing away and recording all that is sung of the song. You are wrong!"

"Who are you?" I sang, "that charges me with wrongness. Cacophony has soiled the seas in all the melodies. He has been the counterpoint to all that delights those who listen to the song. He must die. Who are you, old whale, who stops that which must be?"

A silence pervaded the sea as the old whale lifted with a wave that attempted to wash all things to the shore. "Know you me not, scribe? Has your anger wiped your memory clean? I am Philosophy, the elder of the pod, the dreamer of dreams since the very beginning of the song.

Listen to that which you have been charged with . . . remembering. Remember me in song. Remember that which you have pledged to do. Then do what must be done."

The Song of the Sea began to reel in my mind and heart as I listened to the old man. Cacophony floated nearby, awaiting life or death but seemingly not caring which. I wanted to crush the life from him, but the song sang to me and, as before, I listened. The responsibility for which I was charged was right. Tides before, near the very deep, I had drunk the melody that Tympani had sung. In memory of the melody that I carried in my very soul, I broke off the attack. Sullenly, I dropped deep and reflected on my wrongness. I was to observe and never be involved; that was the song, and that was the only way it could be sung.

I cooled myself in the deep. When I breached, Cacophony was gone, and the seas were quiet still. Far away in the distance, I could hear the pod moving stoically onward in the seas, the event forgotten, to be remembered only by the scribe who was charged with all rememberings. I sang the event of the fight over to myself again and again until the angry tune had become part and parcel of the song. Then, and only then, did I move to rejoin the pod.

Times and tides passed. The song took on a gentle melody, as all events became non-events and monotone. I allowed the memories of my journeys to fade like the mist of past rain days. There were births and deaths and tiny things that became simple notes in a complex song.

Percussion, the ill-fated mate of Cacophony, calved at a time of storm, and the winds whipped the sea into a mighty froth. She breached and dove, breached and dove, through the changing of the tide, groaning and complaining of the child birthing within her. Then, she began the spin of life. Round and round she spun in tighter and

tighter circles, until the momentum itself sent a slick bundle of life spinning too, into the sea.

As long as I live and as long as I sing, I shall always pause at the crescendo of birth. It is magic and power of the most perfect kind. It is violent and possesses a demonic strength like a mighty storm of clashing light. Following the storm always comes the calm, which only heightens the amazement of the birth. Always, there is anguish as the child wishes for his separate soul, as if the mother wished to hold on to that bond. The battle of life is a battle of lives, and from this singularity there comes two: the child fresh and new and the mother forever changed by that which she can share with no one.

Percussion called her calf Progeny, but he was as unlike his father as Cacophony was unlike his own father, Tympani. Progeny became my shadow, a dark dart that flowed in the waters where I swam. As I recorded all that happened, he watched and looked on in innocence and wonder. "Why?" was his byword and the beginning to all that he spoke to me, "Why do we sing?" "Why do we swim?" "Why do sandwalkers walk on the sand?" "Why do they wish us dead?" "Why can't they sing?" "Why has my father forsaken me?"

To all of these questions I could answer with simple song, but to the final question I had no answer. I suppose I could have sung some of the off-colored songs that Cacophony composed. I suppose I could have sung of the death and destruction that he caused, but I didn't. For to sing that verse would have been to alter the song, and Philosophy had brought that message home hard.

There comes a tremendous responsibility with a shadow like Progeny. Many, many times he wrapped himself in the coral kelp that grew in great profusion on all of our journeys. He would always wait patiently for me to unwind him, then, once again, he would slip into my wake and tag along.

Because of the little calf, I interfered one final time. One break of tide, as I wandered far from the main pod to rest my ears from the onslaught of the song, I breached as was my wont and Progeny followed, imitating in his small way my bigger moves. To do a final cleansing of my soul, I dove deep, and Progeny stayed above in the bright silvered light warming himself against the colder waters.

I swam deeper than I had swum in hundreds of tides, and I did not surface for a goodly time. In the deep, I reflected on the song and felt the harmonics of the song as they washed me clean. The pressure, though strong about me, left my spirit clean, and I felt somewhat ful-filled by all that had transpired. So deep was my musing and delight in finding release from my self-imposed torment that, as I slowly lifted from the bottom of the crystal cold dark, I didn't rec-ognize the simple introductions to fear and danger.

I was snapped from my daydreams of self-complacency as there came from the surface a screaming . . . a tiny song of terror. With a mighty thrust of my flukes, I climbed into the warmer waters of the bright side. Above me, sitting still in the rocking waters, were shell-sharks, and within the shells, as always, the sandwalkers.

The remembering happened of other times and other

places, of dolphins caught in nets of kelp and their brutal beatings. My blood ran through my veins and blocked all sense of logic, of responsi-bility to the sacredness of the scribe. I calmed myself, humming bits of the song that would help me in this situation.

Silently, I eased to the waters' surface, and once again there came the non-musical screams of fright, and this time I recognized the singer of that song—Progeny. Twisting this way and that, I sud-denly saw clearly what had transpired. For there, right before me, was my little friend, trapped,

I was surprised that it lifted as easily as it did
but not as surprised as the sandwalkers
who spilled into my domain.

rolled, and caught in a weaving of kelp-like vine. With age comes a certain maturity and that detached ability to slow down before reacting. I breathed deeply of what little air I had left and breached quietly near the shell-sharks and their cargo of sandwalkers.

Other times and in other tunes stored in the song were memories of the sandwalkers, not killing my fellow singers, but literally stealing them from the waters of life. This was what was happening here. The sandwalkers were rolling poor, dear Progeny in their stronger-than-kelp and trying to lift him from the waters. My charge was to stand off and record objectively all that happened to the song, but this bit of melody was one I could not leave alone.

I breathed in those sweet, energy-instilling airs of above and dove deep. Then with bends and kicks of my body and with all muscles in play, I surged up through the sea. With all the power in my body and soul, I rammed into the rocking shell-shark. I was surprised that it lifted as easily as it did but not as surprised as the sandwalkers who spilled into my domain. I charged again and again, ramming all of the shell-sharks until they looked down with large blank stares. With my teeth, I ripped and tore at the stronger-than-kelp and finally, like a slippery eel, Progeny flashed by me in fear and slid to the deep.

Vengeance warmed my blood 'til boiling as I hummed the roaring song of Adagio and remembered other scars of the symphony called Song of the Sea. I breached high from the water and came crashing down on the shell-sharks. Delightfully, I could feel them splinter and break beneath me. Over and over, I breached and broke until there was nothing left to break. Nothing save the sandwalkers themselves. How insignificant they looked from beneath. Pale flipping fins that thrashed and fought at the waters, instead of working with them. I surfaced in their midst, prepared to wreack personal havoc and to take one or two with me to the deep for a long discussion of the wrongs they had committed to those of my kind.

But as I prepared to sing of blood, I remembered the shell-shark with the clouds of kelp and also the little yellow shell that had saved me so long ago. I stopped and stared and looked into the eyes and very soul of a sandwalker. In that momentary gaze, I found bits and pieces of a song. Not our song, but a song just the same. My reverie was broken by the distant drone of other shell-sharks racing from somewhere in the distance. Fearing for my own safety, I slipped back to the waters to find my adopted little brother, Progeny. As I swam away, I waved my fin as if to say goodbye.

DIRGE

We journeyed with the tides and moved about the world. The bright light and night of the silverside moved in an unending blur of activity, all of which was turned to song. It was on the tenth journey that I heard the classical tones of Philosophy once again.

The pod had been moving slowly from the warm waters of birthing to the cold waters of life paralleling the dryside when all stopped.

Philosophy, who seemed as old as the song itself, had lagged far behind. Objectively, I drew away from the main pod to seek out this old whale and see what bit or piece he was creating. What I found was sad indeed—a whale that had grown so old and feeble he was barely able to move. His mind had gentled, and I found his song sung in a monotone. I followed and watched as he moved with deliberation of purpose toward the pod.

After nearly a completed tide, he joined the main body of the pod, but was very inactive, floating near the surface. When asked if all was right, he sang in a reedy voice that he was dreaming of a new theme for the song itself. The pod was patient and took this time to feed heavily on all those sweet things that can be found to eat in the warmer waters.

Early the next day, when the bright lights had overshadowed the night of the silverside, Philosophy began to sing. At first it was only a gentle harmonic rippling the water, but slowly it crescendoed into a demand that all the pod gather about. From all points and depths of the sea, they came. We moved and surrounded this aging whale of wisdom and dreams.

"I am old," he said. "I am about to slip from the waves that rock the sea and fall like a rock to the deep! As is my wont, I wish to reunite myself voluntarily with the waters of life and give up that which was given to me."

The pod buzzed in excitement but quieted again as the old whale continued, "I call upon my rights from the song as sung by the Narwhal of the Horn . . . for the THOUSAND DEATHS OF THE SAND-WALKER." Then in dramatic punctuation, he lay quiet still and rolled with the waves, singing nothing. But from the pod there was a silent expectation of more and a searching for understanding of his request.

My charge was to record all, as part and parcel of the song. While Philosophy sang, I recalled the ghostly pair I had met so long ago who had first sung of the "death." I silently recited my dream-like meeting with the Narwhal and their call for all who would, to throw themselves upon the shore in obscure protest. I tore deep into the heart and soul of the very song itself searching for a melody that would guide me to the understanding of what Philosophy had demanded and if that request should be honored. The pod turned to me and waited in nervous anticipation.

How long they waited or how long I searched I do not know, but suddenly from the very beginnings of the song I found the passage as sung to me by the Narwhal. At first as a gentle humming and then to full voice, I sang, "There will come a time when the song as sung need not be sung any more. There will come a time when one amidst the pod will call for the THOUSAND DEATHS OF THE SANDWALKER, to cast our bodies to the shore in silent protest of all the wrongs the sandwalkers have committed to the sea. The pod must agree, as one, willingly to let this heart and soul give up that which was given. The whale, so honored, will be allowed to lead the pod, and all are to swim to the dryside, there to leave the waters of life forever and die, never to return to the sea.

"But the decision is great for the pod. For, with the honor of the THOUSAND DEATHS OF THE SAND-WALKER, the song must be ended. All must go. All must sing the final song with the one so honored. All must gloriously rush to the shores of the dryside and sing a final stanza to those that wish us gone from the sea. This is not ignominious death, but rather a rapturous crescendo honoring all of those who have swum and still swim the waters of life. So it is sung in the Song of the Sea."

As I finished, the seas were gentle and smooth. The pod floated as if suspended in time and place as I reflected on what I had sung. All, every member of the pod from Progeny to Philosophy, would die the purported honored death. Right or wrong, I knew not which, but a feeling of waste pervaded my very soul. Surely the pod would see the futility in this gesture of ending the song. I was but the scribe. I was the singer of the song and could not, would not, enter the debate as to the value of this decision. I was charged with listening, detached, a part, yet not a part. I waited as all those others waited for a new song to be sung to end the anticipation of this frightful request. Surely Philosophy had grown mad with the aging. Surely the pod would not agree.

Night had come with the rising of the silverside and the melting of the golden bright light. Nothing moved but the waters themselves. The tiny bright flashes of the far above watched and cooled the seas, but no one moved. Everyone, young and old alike, silently sang the song that had been sung.

Then, as the bright light of early morning skipped across the rolling waves like some great silvered fish, the pod began to sing as one. "We greet the morning. We greet the day. We honor those that have gone before. We honor those still living. We now honor Philosophy with the beginning, the end. We gladly go as one to sing the final passage to the Song of the Sea."

As long as I live, as long as I float and swim the seas seeking my destiny, I will hear those hollow lyrics to the song. My mind reeled about as I recorded all, as was my charge. Unexpectedly, I was caught in the excitement, the fever of this momentous occasion and I too began to sing the acquiescence. I hummed, and my blood boiled with the power that comes from such decision. It was done. The pod had decided and the insidious wave began its ominous roll to the shore.

I moved to join the pod's procession but the old, cracked voice of Philosophy cried out, "No, Harmony! All the pod must go as one, save for one . . . the scribe, the sentinel, the singer of the song. You must stand away and record the final notes. You are charged, as you have been charged before, with watching and wanting. There is no other way. When all is done you must sing the song in all its finality to another pod so that the traditions will be passed on. As you sing the final

Night had come with the rising of the silverside
and the melting of the golden bright light.

notes of the song, then will you enjoy the rapture of all that we have enjoyed. Then shall you have your end, your beginning. This is the way it has been. This is the way it shall be."

Silence once again knifed through the pod but was replaced by the blood call of the decision. So numbed was I, that I simply recorded and thought not at all of what would come later.

As the pod sang their song of expectation, I heard, from far away, the angry bellowings of Cacophony as he breached into the skies. "It was mine. The song was mine. Mine to sing. Mine to listen. I agree but disagree. I love but hate. I swim but fly. I do not want to die!" This outburst was heard, like many tunes, only by me. It was followed by silence, as Cacophony sounded deep and disappeared from the song for a time.

The pod did not move; the pod did not sing. I lulled in the waters off the shore and waited for the darkness of the night of the silverside. For this was a time of great madness, as the silverside pulled not only at the tides but twisted our sanity and reason. With the silence and the quiet of the pod, I dropped from the world to reflect on the fullness of the song. The music of all the histories reeled in my mind as I sought some form of escape from the decision of Philosophy. The music whispered like a quick wind that blows, but no remedy came.

I remembered that over time other scribes had touched the pod. They had come in their anguish of being alone and to sing their song one more time. When finished, as they sang the final glory of all that was the thousand deaths, they became one with the sea, their song echoing forever in the song of the new pod. Then and only then, could they die their quiet death. For being a scribe without song is an emptiness that is the end, the beginning.

I remembered that, once upon a tide, one scribe came not alone. He came with a mate. As this scribe from some unknown, long-departed pod sang, his mate joined in gentle harmony to all that was in their song. At the final crescendo, they ended all together. I could take a mate!

It was always known to me that I could take a wife, and it was always assumed that in some tide, Melody and I would be one. Now was my final chance to join, to have a companion to ease the lonely tides as I searched for a pod to pass the song along. A mate. An interlude in my personal song in which I could reflect and join and become one for a time. No time for calving, no time for child, but still something to grasp in my journey to the end. Without thinking, I breached and called loudly for Melody. Her name echoed about the pod as they floated idly in deep contemplation of all that was, and was to be.

The waters seemed to sweeten as I felt her come near, her song questioning, yet demanding. The wind whipped at the waves and froth, in the form of tiny bubbles lifted in the air reflecting the lavenders and blues of the twinkling lights overhead. She sang a gentle blush and brushed against me as the swell of the waters lifted us both in unison. We became one for a moment, there in the brilliance of the reflected silver light, and for that moment, forgotten was the world.

The forgetting seemed forever. There was no yesterday, only the sweet promise of now, but like the tides that roll in and out, tomorrow crept upon us. What had been only two in the world, became all things of the sea, and a pod that demanded to sing a fatal song. I came to my senses.

"Stay with me Melody," I crooned. "As is my right as scribe for a pod that seeks to end its song, be my mate. Stay with me and listen to this strange glory. Our tides will not be long, but we can see what we can, as we seek another pod to sing our final song."

She sang nothing for a time as we rode the crest of the silverside tide, then slowly, she pulled away.

In answer, Melody slowly was moved from my side by the tide of the night of silverside. "Let me think," she cried as she swam quickly away. "Let me think of that which I should do."

I found myself alone, wrapped in my own self-effacing song. Pity always wraps those that sing of it, in a numbing blanket of false warmth and security. I heard not the seas, nor the simple tunes sung by the others that swam the waters of life. I could only hear my own song as I lamented a love lost.

So dulled was I by my saddened introspection, it was a long time before I realized that something was very wrong indeed. I felt the waters begin to churn as I was tossed this way and that. Blinking my eyes in confusion, shaking off the lethargy that had enveloped me, I was tossed again violently as a giant fluke smashed me full in the face.

I turned and looked but could see nothing. Then, coming from the murkiness of the depths was a shape and form I knew only too well— Cacophony! His eyes were glazed and shot with the rage of the hot blood that coursed in his veins. Full into my side, he hammered, and I felt the bone and cartilage splinter and crush. I twisted in slow agony trying to hold on to conscious thought, but the darkness of the night was getting darker, and I could not react as he struck, again and again.

I floated, unable to defend myself, all the sweet dryside airs driven from my body. I could only listen as Cacophony railed, "Die, white whale, die. Die not the honorable THOUSAND DEATHS OF THE SANDWALKER, but die just the same. You have taken the song that should have been mine.

"I don't know, Harmony. I feel I must sing with those I have sung with always. Philosophy has called for the final song and of that honor I, too, will sing. But, I also feel for your song. I long to sing both songs."

"But," I protested, "it seems so futile, such a waste of life and the song. We have lived, frolicked, and swum the seas. We have run from dangers. Have we survived only to drown in the dryside? What makes Philosophy right? What makes the death of all for the death of one so glorious? Who has a right to ask us to give up our world for the sake of an old whale's pride? Don't sing with them, sing with me!"

You have changed my life. You have made all the wrongs seem right. You may have the honor to stand aside and listen as we all sing the final song, but I take that honor away. I take back that which you have taken from me!"

He receded into the gloom, and I could barely discern his form as he prepared to deal the final blow. As he charged, I steeled myself for the end, the beginning. Just as he was about upon me, a tiny form leaped through the waters and deflected his blow. Like a dolphin, darting here and there, was Progeny. Progeny, my tiny friend, was no match for this monster of the deep but attack he did.

"You must leave him be!" Progeny sang in his child-whale voice. "You must be gone from the crystal seas." He rammed the much larger whale square in the eye, and Cacophony was blinded on one side. Progeny darted this way and that, and before Cacophony could react, this silvery missile smacked into his other side, rendering the mad bull totally blind.

"My son," croaked Cacophony in shock and disbelief, "you would side with him that has taken the song from your father?"

"Yes," cried Progeny, "I learned from Harmony to give all for the song."

"And, I suppose," continued the blinded whale in gentler tones now, "that dear, sweet Harmony has sung all sorts of ditties about your father. I suppose he has sung in a loud voice all the wrong that he felt I had done."

"No, father. Harmony has not sung of you at all. He has avoided all melodies with mention of you for fear of turning me against you. No, father, the song I sing is one of observation. I have watched. I have listened. You are not good for the sea!"

Cacophony paused in silence as he thought on all that had been spoken. Then, he softly spoke,

"May chance you are right, my son. May chance I have squandered the wealth that the waters of life gave me. Oh, I am so sorry. I have not been a father to you at all. I have ignored you and I know not your song. Come closer so that I may see you, for you have blinded my eyes and I can barely see."

As Cacophony spoke, the child's angry resolve softened and then turned quickly to pity and shame. "Father," cried the tiny whale as he cautiously slipped to Cacophony's side, "I have hurt you so, but I only did so to save another."

Progeny moved near to his father and began to sing a song of gentle healing, as he brushed against the eyes that could not see. Round and round, round and round, he wove about the injured whale, as he tried to soothe the injuries that he had caused.

Suddenly, the older whale twisted his massive body and with one mighty blow, smashed his tail with all of his weight into the tiny whale.

I could not interfere.
I could not be involved.

With a burst of bubbles, Progeny softly sang, "Father, why?"

"Why? why?" his father laughed, "You are my son, and you have to ask why? Anyone who dares to strike at the mighty Cacophony shall not live long in the sea. Adagio, the fat whale; Tympani, my learned father; Harmony, the great white; even you, my son, none shall live that fail to understand—I am he that controls the

sea." And with a crash of body on body and a cackle of laughter, Cacophony ended the just-begun life of his son, Progeny.

I lay there still in the water. "Oh, my dear sweet child, Progeny. Yours was a special gift of laughter and mischief. Yours was always to give to me, and now you are gone, involved in that which you did not belong!"

My lament was broken again by the discordant voice of Cacophony, "Now, white whale, as my vision clears, we shall finish that which is ours to finish." He began moving towards me and I once again steeled myself for the end. Droning a senseless tune, he moved in the ever-tightening circle of the death spin. I had just begun to sing my final song, to quietly ease what pain was coming, when Cacophony stopped.

The waters surrounding us were filled with such frothing that as single-minded as was his intent, he stopped. But the water wasn't truly frothing. The waters were dancing with the unified voices of all the pod, singing the first chorus to the Song of the Sea, the prelude to the death of Philosophy. The notes of the song were accented by each of the pod, from the smallest to the largest, and it caught them all in a fever

of finale. Whale by whale, they breached between Cacophony and me, and whale by whale, they separated us. Cacophony bellowed in rage, but no one in the pod reacted, for the ritual had begun. "Stop!" he cried, "I am Cacophony. I will not lower myself to the clamshell level of you . . . you followers! I am the leader."

But the pod as one ignored him and pushed him to shore behind the slowly swimming, age-mad Philosophy.

Cacophony began to panic as he realized he was trapped at the head of the procession. "You kelp heads, you crusty-coated feathered furies, let me be! I should have been the scribe. The song should have been mine to sing."

But the pod continued to sing as one. The mad bull tried vainly to swim through the pod and back out to sea, but the crush of whales was so massive that in their fervor, they would not let him go. He battered and slammed at the moving wall of flesh but they were resolute in their determination. All the while, Philosophy moved through the break line of the crashing waves, closer and closer to shore as he hummed a sweet gentle tune in counterpoint.

As the pod passed me by, so did Melody, and the waters seemed saltier still as rainbow-hued tears welled in her eyes. "I love you, Harmony. I want that noted and reflected in this, the final crescendo of the song. I wish I could stay. I wish I could live a moment more with you by my side, but the tradition is compelling. I will be with you forever in song."

I was injured and could do nothing but listen. I floated in the sea, charged with the responsibility of those things that had been sung before. I could not interfere. I could not be involved. I was the scribe . . . the singer of the song. I was to listen and to remember, not necessarily of choice but rather by chance alone.

The pod moved by and I was left alone in a sea awash with the music of the honor and vengeance of the THOUSAND DEATHS OF THE SANDWALKER. I heard and remembered tens and hundreds of individual litanies as the pod moved where the waves broke upon the sands. I heard simple tunes of love lasting forever, and mothers cheering their children, and the children nervously responding, not truly understanding all this stuff of traditions. I listened as Cacophony bellowed, at first in rage and then in total fear, for his end was very near. Though he thrashed and tried to force himself back to sea, the press of flesh was too much, and he was rolled in the waves that crashed closer and closer to the shore.

All the pod was embroiled in personal notes, all of which became part and parcel to the final singing of the song. At the head of this senseless procession was Philosophy, and slowly I began to isolate his ending song. I expected something deep and meaningful but instead I heard a silly lullaby, a song a mother would sing to a child. His sing-song voice rocked with the waves as his ancient form began to grate on the sand. This was not the tune of some great member of the pod. This was the song of a whale gone mad. This tradition, this death of the sandwalkers, was the whim and wish of senility. It was off tune.

The sea now rang with other noises, the rattle and grating clackings of the sandwalkers as the shore filled with their scores. Why were they here? Why would they mingle with us? Why would they interfere with the song as it was sung in all its glory?

Finally, I began to realize that in a way maybe Cacophony was right, and all of this was senseless waste and carp bile. I started to move my aching limbs and began to shake myself from the lethargy of this tradition. This was wrong! This hideous act must be stopped! Waste, what a waste, all the pod, all the lives thrown to the shore to end all, to honor some whale who now sang of chasing tuna-tails and butterflies. I pushed my way through the massive slick flesh that blindly moved to a sandy death.

"Stop," I cried, "Go back. This, what you do, is wrong! Stop the singing, stop the song! The final test is the sanity, the rightness, of him who calls for the death. Philosophy is not right with the world. He has failed the test. This death should not be!" But my pleas fell on ears deafened by that which has happened before. As I tried to turn the tide and force them back to sea, some were already singing their final melody. I pushed and shoved, bit and battered at them, but they would not be dissuaded. Back and forth, my belly dragging upon the sand as my great fin stood from the water like some sagging white sail, I swam, trying to stop all from this stupidity. The waters frothed about me as I sought Melody. Surely she would listen to the logic of all this insanity.

Voices began to drop out from the song as they transpired and were gone forever. I lashed at some, battered at others—anything to get somebody's attention. Some of the babies, the smaller whales, frightened by my machinations, moved miraculously back from the shore, but it was all I could do to keep them away from the death, for they did not understand, wanting only to be near their mothers. Mixed in with the rocking bodies of all the pod were the hideous, frail sandwalkers who strangely waded in the waters with us.

Before me, closer to the shore, I could hear the beautiful bell-like sounds of my beloved Melody, as she reached the goal. "No!" I bellowed. "Do not die, my sweet. You can live. This final song is a lie. It should not be sung." I flipped and pulled at these waterless sands forcing myself higher and higher into the dryside and closer to my Melody. I must save her. I must force her back into the waters of life, back to sensibility.

As I pushed forward, I felt myself being pushed back. Not by the sea, which was rushing to the shore, but by the dry-skinned fins of the sandwalkers. "Let me be!" I sang, but as I noted before, these strange creatures know not how to sing, and worse still, would not listen to my song. I fought against them. I pushed and twisted and hammered myself closer to my love, my life itself. They pulled; I pushed.

Then to my horror, I heard the final, gloriously dreadful sound of Melody singing her last. She sang the song of love, the song of my life as she saw it. She sang a song of calves not born and the golden light we would never see again.

"I loved you, Harmony," she sang. "I loved you then; I love you now, and I dedicate my end, my beginning to you!" And with that, the waves seemed to stop and the seas went flat. The song ended. The song was no more to be. For the first time in my life, I heard a silent world, a world without a song.

I paused in my grief and stared with great unblinking eyes at the shore that was now strewn with the bodies, the hulks of all that I had loved and come to know. How long I lay there, I do not know. I felt myself at some other time being pressed back to the sea by the strange sandwalkers. But I cared not, idly floating and allowing the waves to move me to the shore. Now I too had reason to die, for I had no reason to live. The song that I had been charged with singing was a flat buzzing sound of memory only. It was then that all around me faded to black and cooler greys.

CODA

I remembered nothing for a tide or tides, I know not which. I stirred as one waking from a frightful sleep. I stretched and my body ached. I looked about and found that I was close to the breakers and a little way from the shore. I listened, but there was no song.

I knew that what I had hoped I had dreamed, was real. I was alone with the memory of the Song of the Sea.

The memory. Of all that is holy, the memory! The whales were dead! My mind was flooded with memory. The delights, the laughters, the fears. To remember was to ache with such gut-wrenching pain that to think was effort, not worth the price. I twisted in my own sea of guilt as I wondered the impact of my singing of the Narwhal song. I agonized my journey and the singing of that song. How much of all of this was my own responsibility? How much guilt was mine truly earned?

How deep was my conceit at the wonder of the song. How hollow is a song when there is no one to sing it to. Now, being scribe was not an honor. Now, being scribe was charged with the horrible prospect of passing this hideous rite on to another pod, as it had been passed on to us. Others—and still others—would die, and like those interwoven nets of kelp, it would keep building until all the seas would be silent forever.

"No!" I screamed, "This will end with me. This will end forever here. I will join the others in their futility, rather than take the chance that this song might be sung again."

Slowly, I turned my back to the sea and returned to the dryside. I began to sing of recrimination. I was the one who returned from the journey and passed on the hatred of the sandwalker. I was the one who had listened to the dreams of the Narwhal and passed on their vengeance to the pod.

"The pod. The pod." I cried again and again. Then, with the speaking of the word, came fresh memory anew, and like a sharp-fin, it ripped at my heart and devoured my soul.

"Melody and Progeny, my own sweet mother, Rhapsody, all are dead," I wailed, and the tears blurred my vision of purpose so that I could not see. A wave lifted me higher and threw me closer to the shore and to the end I so desperately sought. The coral sand began to scrape along my belly; still I fought higher and higher, up the land shelf into the dryside. Finally, I could swim no more and was beached like a monstrous log in the land of the sandwalkers.

With a calmness that belied my spirit, I sang of other days. I sang loudly so the Song of the Sea

momentarily snapped me from my private wake, for no feathered fury could pull a whale back to the sea. What was it?

"Ah, no matter," I mused out loud. "It matters not at all whether it is a feathered fury, or a great sharp-fin pulling me into the sea as a meal. It matters not, for the song is dead."

Suddenly, my self-pitying reverie was broken by excited chitterings and a voice that sang from out of the past, "You blubber-brain. Help us for pity's sake!"

"Help us? Help who?" I asked deliriously.

I heard my own words being mimicked like an echo gone bad, "Help us? Help who? Help me? Help you? Come on, pudge butt, help yourself." My brain was fogged with grief, but still and all, echoes don't add to words spoken. Echoes don't speak in squeaky voices. Then the voices were remembered—Little Brother and Laughter Ring.

"Let me die!" I cried. "For the song is silent, and the pod is dead!" I pulled from their grasp

would be carried on the winds of the dryside, and all the sandwalkers could hear what I had done—what they had done—what we all had done to the world. I sang of destruction. I sang of the lives lost and the friends departed. I waited for the end . . . the beginning.

As I lay there prepared for death and embroiled in my own self-pity, I felt a biting, a pulling at my tail. "Odd," thought I, "already the feathered furies are pulling at my flesh." But what monstrous feathered furies! These strange furies not only pulled at me, they yanked. I felt myself being scraped backward. The oddity of this event and once again began inching my way back up the shore, but once again I was held short of my goal. "By all things that are holy, let me die! For all is lost!"

"Not quite all," shouted Little Brother, yanking me rudely again toward the sea. "For out in the deep wait the children that you saved. Did you save them only to let them die of neglect and confusion?"

I paused in my struggle, and far out to sea I could hear the gentle, tiny squeaks of the babies. All in the pod were not dead. I remembered in a rush that in my madness to break the spell of death I had pushed several young whales back to the deep. Now, with no one to guide them, they floated and called to the others that could not hear.

But obstinacy is born of pride, and I shook their simple songs from my ears and would not listen. "No!" I bellowed. "I am whale, and my right is to die as the others before."

Suddenly, my friends from long ago, let go. "Fine," taunted Laughter Ring, "and the Narwhal are right as they sing. But what happens when there are no more whales? What happens when all the whales have cast themselves upon the shore? Do you think the sandwalker will feel your protest after you are gone? No! They will push your fat, rotting carcass back to the sea or better still, leave it where it lies. Then they will quickly forget and continue with their ruination of the world."

"But," I protested weakly, "I have carried out my responsibility. I have sung the song."

"That's carp bile, and you know it," snapped Little Brother. "Who do you sing to as you die? Do you sing to the children, so they can continue this madness? Or do you sing to the sandwalker? There is good reason why the sandwalker does not sing the Song of the Sea. For how can you sing that which you cannot hear?"

I froze in my undulations to reach the dryside. I paused. Perhaps they were right. The sandwalker does not sing our song, and we, the whale, can't sing his. With a sigh breathed deep, I exhaled all that was wrong with my soul and began slowly to turn back to the sea.

I flipped and flopped, helping my friends to extricate me from the shore, and slowly inched my painful way from the sands of the dryside. The salty waters of life burned my wounds but, all in all, soothed my dry skin. As my wounds tingled with the sharp bite of healing, I dropped into the deep to soothe that tortured melody echoing in my mind. My little friends let me be while I mused my situation. The children must learn the Song of the Sea, and from its singing would come change. All must learn the song, not only whale but flipper-fin and dolphin. All of the waters of life must sing the same, not bits of melody here and there.

While there, on the bottom of the world as I knew it, I found answers that had never been questioned. For there was a way to protest the sandwalker. There was a way to remove the sandwalker for all time from the sea. Exalted with rebirth and buoyant with the spirit that has made the whale strong for all of time, I breached. For the first time, for the last time, I breached for the life of all living creatures in the sea.

Sustained by the new life within me and aided by my dear friends, we searched for the children of tomorrow. We found them not far from shore, confused and so alone. There were seven in all. They sang to us for guidance. They asked for the song, and they asked for food. Fortunately, all but one of them had tried the first taste of fish and needed not their mothers' milk. Little Brother, Laughter Ring, and I swam ourselves ragged, hunting fish and returning to feed the hungry mouths that waited, still confused but soothed by the food.

Though we tried to feed the littlest one, she was so distraught she would not eat the fish we offered and cried fitfully for the warmth of her mother's milk. "What are we to do?" I asked of the others, "I can soothe the young ones with the song and feed them with the fish, but this little one I can do nothing for."

"It has been done before," Laughter Ring said quietly. "We are both of the family of the sea. I will nurse the young one until she can be taught to eat the fish. It may not be much, but it will have to do."

"That's ridiculous," snorted Little Brother. "You can't nurse another unless you are great with child." He paused and looked foolishly at his mate. "Are you? Are we with child?"

Laughter Ring laughed true to her name, "I don't know about you, but I am. If you haven't noticed these last many tides, I have been growing large with child."

Sure enough, I now noticed that Laughter Ring was filled with child, and it was easy to see that she would have no trouble nursing a young one, even a whale.

"But, but," stuttered Little Brother, "I thought you were just getting a little fat. I mean, I thought you were eating a bit more than I . . ."

"Hmm," muttered Laughter Ring, as she sought out the child. "You and I shall talk of this another time. Fatter indeed."

Later, when the silverside replaced the golden light with its silvered reflections, we fed ourselves. Sated, we dozed, rocking on the now gentle seas. I would sleep for a time, then wake abruptly, thinking I had heard Melody's song calling to me from the dryside. After listening for a time and hearing only the gentle rush of the sea falling on the sea, I would fall back into my fitful sleep.

For many tides we moved the small pod around in no particular direction, as all seemed to wait for some pronouncement from me. I paused during the daily hunts to reflect on all of the evil that the sandwalker had done to the sea. I thought of personal things that I would wish to do to one, fifty, and a thousand if they came to me. The havoc I could wreak! But there were so many of them, and my plan must be set in motion that would stop them for all time. My blood never cooled.

Finally, one crystal tide as the golden light crept over the edge of the sea, I began to sing, "The Narwhal are wrong; death is a silent and stupid protest. The Narwhal hide within their frozen crystal walls and give gifts of hate to any whale who happens by, and, one by one, the whale is disappearing. The Narwhal could do no better if they all gave their twisted horns to the sandwalker, so that they could kill even more of us in the seas.

They must be stopped and a new song must be sung. Not a song sung by just a single pod of whale, here or there, but all in one massive chorus. And the new song will not be sung by just the whale but by all of the brethren, the dolphins and the flipper-fin—all must learn to sing the same song. And, united, the voice of all shall be strong.

For I have a plan, a simple plan indeed, that will put an end to the sandwalker as ALL THAT IS RIGHT IN THE WORLD intended when the sandwalkers were cast upon the dryside.

I shall call a conclave, the greatest meeting of all the brethren of the sea. There shall we sing. There shall be the beginning, the end of the sandwalker forever. Go now, my friends. Call your group of dolphins together, and each one of that group shall go to another and another group, to tell of the conclave. Call to the flipper-fin and the great-backed whale. Call to the blue and the bow head. We shall all meet in five hundred tides in the crystal walls of the Narwhal of the Horn."

For the first time, for the last time,
I breached for the life
of all living creatures in the sea.

Little Brother had tears in his eyes, "We shall be three when we meet again: Laughter Ring, our baby, and me. Worry not of us, we shall carry the invitation to sing to all that have the will to hear." With that brief farewell and promises to meet in the cold, icy waters, they swam quickly away.

As the waters rippled around them in wake, I could still hear Laughter Ring cheerfully chide her mate, "You thought I was fat? In all my years, I will never be as fat as your head, you bait fish."

I watched as they swam from view, my heart aching for what we had shared, but soon we would share again in dreams. For in the chance of dreams lies the hope for tomorrow. Reluctantly, I turned my little pod up into the sea, moving slowly to the cold waters, to answer all the questions yet unasked of my plan to destroy the sandwalker and his evil ways. We would search for the Narwhal, and once found, stop their song forever, and give them the new.

For it is my song to sing that the world shall become whole again. The seas shall become one with the land, and the land, one with the sea. The song that is sung by ALL THAT IS RIGHT IN THE WORLD shall be sung by all.

I sing to you as I sing to me—this the Song of the Sea. I am Harmony, the last whale of my kind. All the rest of my pod are dead and gone. If you can hear the song as it is sung, you must sing it to another and another, so all the whales and dolphins that have died shall not have died in vain.

As this is the end, so it is the beginning.

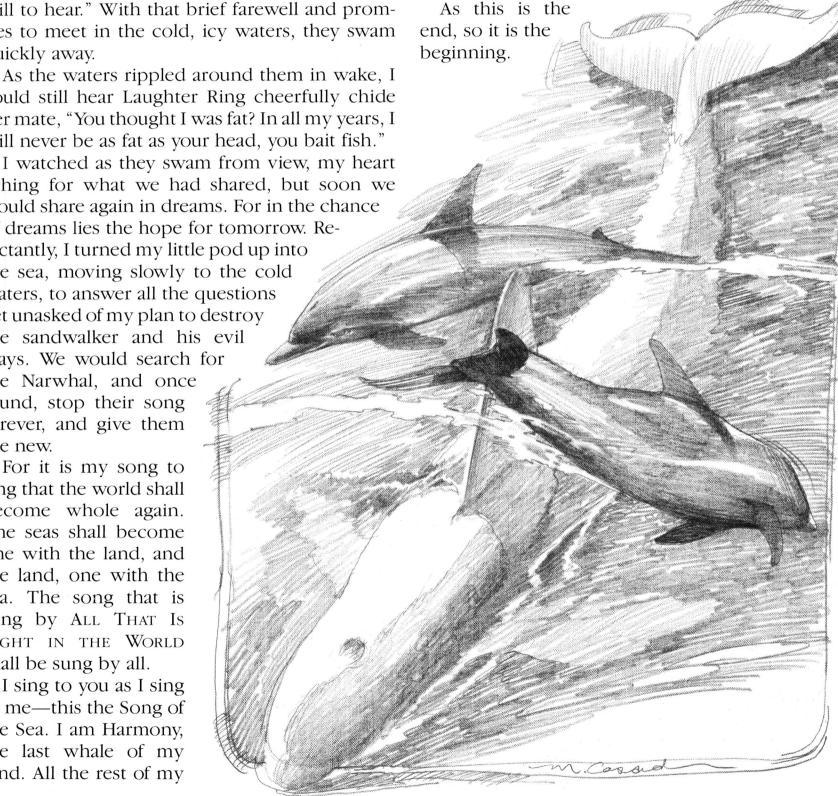